MORE PRAISE FOR *UNDERJUNGLE*

"What can I say about *Underjungle* but *Oh my God*. So, so gorgeously strange, told by a sea creature, and set completely underwater, *Underjungle* (even the title is fantastic) is about all the big issues—love, loss, family, war—but it's also about how all the oceans, like all of us, are connected—and the dangers when we forget that, and it's written in prose as startlingly beautiful as the discovery of a real pearl shimmering in an oyster. A love letter to our oceans, *Underjungle* glints with humor and heart, and it's totally unlike anything you've ever read before."
—Caroline Leavitt, author of *With or Without You*

"*Underjungle* isn't just a novel. It's a symphonic meditation on existence, heartache, and underwater worlds beyond our imaginings. In prose both witty and elegiac, Sturz's finned narrator plunges readers into the ocean's depths, evoking such vivid tastes, textures, and scents that they may find themselves reluctant to come up for air."
—Jennifer Steil, author of *Exile Music* and *The Ambassador's Wife*

"James Sturz has written a strange and beautiful book that defies the usual categories. It's a love story, a war story, and undersea epic and a meditation on the human hand. By the time you finish it you will know a lot more about what is happening in the sea around us—which may be the most important story of our time."
—John Benditt, author of *The Boatmaker*

"This love song to the unseen life of the ocean is a thing of passion, beauty, and shimmering fish. Deep inside James Sturz's singular and engaging story, there's a message for us who dwell on land: Not just to take care of the ocean, but of one another as well."
—Daphne Merkin, author of *22 Minutes of Unconditional Love*

"*Underjungle* is a wondrously beautiful tale told in language that made me feel I was breathing the atmosphere of an exotic and miraculous planet. Of course, I was. But the most amazing thing is that, the whole time, I was breathing underwater."
—Carl Safina, author of *Song for the Blue Ocean* and *Beyond Words*

"Reality, it has been said, is the aggregate of all perceptions, not just our human ones. The wondrously original *Underjungle* affords the reader rich access to just such perceptions, to a vivid inhuman world. And yet I marveled at the deep sensation of feeling more human for having read it, and have relished, long after the last page, the rock of the waves in my bones."
—Chris Dombrowski, author of *The River You Touch*

"A beautifully written, unique novel that contemplates many of life's big questions as it intrigues and entertains. A delightful read set deep in the ocean, in a part of our planet we're just beginning to understand."

—Bernie Chowdhury, author of *The Last Dive*

"James Sturz creates a world so colorful, imaginative, and diverse that it could only exist within the waters of Planet Ocean. It brings us into intimate contact with a wildly strange, incredible, and yet familiar imagining of aquatic life—and it takes us on a fascinating poetic journey that's a joy to read and will make you love the ocean even more. *Underjungle* is a script for weaving dreams."

—Paul Watson, founder of the *Sea Shepherd Conservation Society* and the *Captain Paul Watson Foundation*

"As a reader, I love to have my mind blown. James Sturz does this in his singular *Underjungle*, an entire novel told from the point of view of fish. Fish! And unknown sea creatures! With great authority, Sturz is able to capture it all: love, loss, heartbreak, danger. I unwittingly learned so much about ocean life, another world, similar but also different than our own."

—Marcy Dermansky, author of *Hurricane Girl*

"Not many of us would have the audacity to write a novel where the only human character is a corpse decomposing on the ocean floor, but in *Underjungle* James Sturz has met this challenge in dazzling fashion. To get a more intimate view of the world under the waves, you'd have to become fish food yourself, so instead I recommend this profound and unclassifiable novel, a mind-expanding *Aeneid* of the seas."

—Ned Beauman, author of *Venomous Lumpsucker*

"James Sturz is the Jacques Cousteau of storytelling. In *Underjungle*, he has crafted a magical, mystical, almost mythological narrative unlike anything else I know, an undersea morality tale for our hurt kind struggling through this postlapsarian mess we made."

—William Giraldi, author of *Hold the Dark* and *Busy Monsters*

"An artistic romp in the underwater world, showing us that humanity barely scratches the surface of understanding our water planet. What a fascinating read!"

—Jill Heinerth, author of *Into the Planet: My Life as a Cave Diver*

"It's OK to eat fish/ 'cause they don't have any feelings,' warbled Kurt Cobain, verbalizing the disconnection many humans have from sea creatures and their vast ocean home. But fish and other critters in *Underjungle* definitely have *feelings*—and opinions!—on love, life, tribal affiliations, and the perplexing visitation from an alien being. James Sturz's narrator is a charismatic, poetic, sometimes snarky guide to exploring the ocean and its denizens in a wholly original way."

—Erica Gies, author of *Water Always Wins*

"In this strange and engaging dystopian novel, Sturz poses more questions than answers. Life beneath the sea may strike most of us as peaceful and serene, but *Underjungle*'s invented underwater realm is surprisingly violent—an echo of the world above?"

—Virginia Morell, author of *Animal Wise* and *Becoming a Marine Biologist*

"*Underjungle* is unlike anything I've ever read: a feverish tale told feverishly by one of the sea's inhabitants. It's a story that will devour you as you devour it, a terrifying tale of war and peace beneath the waves and a paean to the natural underwater beauty that exists without our noticing. It will break your heart, even as it implicates you, lashing you against the coral and feeding you to the sharks. I'm in awe of James Sturz's ravishing, sun-lit, ink-black book full of mesmerizing characters who come to life on the page and resonate with you long after you've read the last word. You're going to love this book and its astonishing conclusion."

—David Samuel Levinson, author of *Tell Me How This Ends Well*

"An otherworldly romance full of poetry and wisdom. I love this novel—a strange, beautiful, and wholly original book. To read James Sturz's *Underjungle* is to be enchanted."

—Iris Smyles, author of *Droll Tales*

AN UNNAMED PRESS BOOK

Copyright © 2023 by James Sturz

Published in North America by the Unnamed Press.

www.unnamedpress.com

Unnamed Press, and the colophon, are registered trademarks
of Unnamed Media LLC.

Hardcover ISBN: 978-1-951213-75-6
Ebook ISBN: 978-1-951213-93-0
LCCN: 2023935194

Cover design and typeset by Jaya Nicely

Manufactured in the United States of America by Sheridan

Distributed by Publishers Group West

First Edition

UNDERJUNGLE

A NOVEL

JAMES STURZ

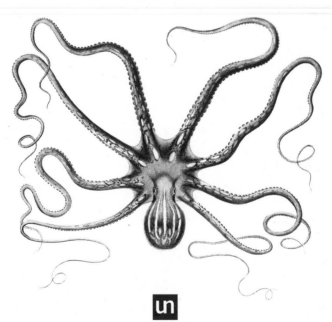

un

The Unnamed Press
Los Angeles, CA

For Paula

All the little fish of her laughter fled
before the shark of her awakening rage.

—Yehuda Amichai

UNDERJUNGLE

Part 1

1

I fell for you from far away. You had skin like waves. I know it wasn't the pull of the moon. You smelled like fresh water, pureness, and trouble amid the pulverized sand and shells. I already knew what you looked like and how you moved.

I was a puddle in the ocean. I wanted to turn you into jelly.

There has never been a world like ours: a place that was perfect even before I knew you were in it. Our world is canyons and ledges and phosphorescent trickles, and mountains and swirls and sponges. It is plankton thick enough for farmers to herd and fissures that flash-boil lobsters into feasts. It is polyps and oysters and undulating pelvic fins. It is our origin and the future. Amid the bleats and yowls, the sea fills quickly with ballads about satisfying every kind of hunger, not all of them requiring food.

I was flailing fins, a somersault of nerves. Hints of you washed across me, and I opened my mouth. There were bubbles in my stomach. I kept reminding myself to breathe.

I've always said this is a peaceful world. There is no stillness. No possibility of getting caught in a morass. What choice is there but to let the current take you? We urge our young to go with the flow. Within the surge and saturation, the hold of water is all around us. To know someone is to engulf them.

Eventually, the tide will bring you back.

This is the only place I know, but it is one of vastness. Of roiling sands and squeals and moans, of thick seaweed forests, abyssal plains and hills and lava pillars coated with volcanic glass. But it is also a cradle. This womb is everywhere. It is a place you never have to leave.

Deep below the surface, our world is cold, dark, and content. Colors are fickle. Red disappears first as you descend, followed by the yellow of the sun. The hundred shades of blue last the longest, but eventually there is only black—and the candied ooze of the ocean floor. Where the pressure is constant, it clings to you as an embrace. We are most comfortable there, in our sheath. But sometimes we'll approach the surface to see the spectacle of lightning strike, and it's a dangerous kind of ecstasy. From the right distance, you feel the water tingle. Closer up, you see and hear the zooplankton fry.

The world is flitters and ripples and secret vibrations. It is languorous undulations and scarlet bellies. When I first sensed you across the ocean, I knew I wanted to make you spill your eggs, so that my gentle army of warriors would attack them.

We are creatures of love, of amorous frenzy. Our tongue-like bodies turn each other into Antarctic slush. Our males flaunt and wiggle their fins in the most ardent ways, then press themselves ferociously against their mates. But when you bear a thousand eggs, you know it's because nearly all of them will die. The sadness of love is unshakable for us. Only the sea cucumbers—so soft and round, and then swelling and stiffening as you knead them, before finally spurting from one end in delirious spasms—exist in a world of sweet, euphoric ignorance.

When our children grow, we urge them to stick together. We make sure they understand their brothers and sisters are not their dinner. It is violence to kill another creature, but it is a necessary violence. The choice not to kill is surely the one to die. When our young decide this (as they sometimes do), it is hard to mourn, since it is a great dishonor to the parents, who expended the time and effort needed to raise them. You can only hope the child grew sufficiently fat and muscled before making the decision to become another animal's food.

But there are different kinds of killing. To watch a cookiecutter shark carve a hole into a wahoo's flank so that it can immediately start feasting on its squishy innards is to witness a peculiar form of ghastliness. But many sharks eat their brothers and sisters before they are born, so what do you expect? I'd rather not think about tilapia in the ocean's farthest reaches, where the water turns brackish, whose females brood their young in their mouths, while bachelor males suck them out and swallow them in a single decimating kiss. And yet those barbarians still leave the female's tongue attached, so the mothers can wail about their losses.

When an animal bleeds from its mouth, you know its tongue and gums and cheeks will soon become a feast for many, so perhaps it is more discreet to enter through its side, although I would not like to experience this myself.

We urge our young to make friends with animals of sufficient size. Make friends with animals with tentacles, but do not always trust them. Make friends with ones without tentacles, but don't expect them to be of much use. Make friends with ones with rotating eyes, because they will always be able to look themselves in the face. But mostly we tell our young never to worry about getting lost, for they'll always be guided by the smell and taste of the water and the irresistible pull of the electromagnetic field. They'll be drawn back home. As I was to you.

Sodium chloride. Magnesium chloride. Agitation. Magnesium sulfate. Calcium sulfate. Potassium sulfate. Fear. Exuberance. Boron. Sadness. Copper. Zinc sulfide. Gold. Each of them maps an unmistakable trail.

You can smell your prey and feel its vibrations in the water. The same is true for someone you desire.

Sometimes a partner will say, "I need space." But we live in unlimited space. How can't you already have all the space you need? If you do need more, where are you supposed to go?

Our movements look brooding, but even we are surprised by our speed. It doesn't take long to cross the universe, to seek out warmer waters for a few days and make a meal of the local *tropicalia*. If those fish don't want to be eaten, why are they so brightly colored, in all those bite-me hues? Life can't all be about preening and flaunting in the hope for a little sex. The flounders know about humility. Many toadfish are open to earnest conversation. Sometimes there is sense to burying yourself in the sand. And yet when I saw you swimming with that school of anchovies around your neck, I was hypnotized. You never said how long it took to train them. I know you wanted to bring them back from the Coral Sea, but they fled our colder waters. At least you still had your oyster shells. You'd balance them across your chest.

"Camouflage," you'd say.

We undulate and flitter about. There are coquettish things some females do with their pelvic fins. To see our younger ones practicing this in groups is at once amusing and upsetting. When the humpbacks start to sing—not those lower moans and thrums, but the deepwater booming, whistling, and yelping—their chants are thrilling and infectious, bouncing through the currents and coursing through the dark. When you hear their songs, how can't you feel your body shake? How do you resist jiggling your booty like a sea lamprey sucking at a salmon's skin?

Their songs vibrate the twilight zone with eddying bursts of light.

We are acrobatic and lithe and quick to alter course with the minutest flick of a single fin. Only my childhood guardian, Gola,[*] is the exception. With the grievous wound to his swim bladder, he keeps rising and sinking uncontrollably. We've all seen him shoot up awkwardly in the middle of a conversation.

"My injury," he says, "makes me ridiculous. Everyone says I have trouble staying on point."

Only fragments of soft coral float up. Intelligent life is better known for attempts at depth.

Once a month, we visit the tomb, our prayer house in the canyon. Encrusted with urchins and mottled with calcium carbonate, magnesium hydroxide, and iron-manganese oxide, it is a magnificent figure. We've all heard the whales gulp and drone as they pass. Ribs rise in aching columns from the floor, like ancient hydrothermal vents. Its vertebrae are shattered chunks. The massive caudal fin sits a quarter league away. No one admits to having played hide-and-seek in the body as a child, but it is what we all remember and it is what we think. Some claim this place isn't truly sacred. There are places

[*]Golā'ynī'shlz'era.

where the water is too cold and deep. They say, *That* is God. *That* is the afterlife. *That* is heaven. But to see the remnants of this beast—this thing that turns blue whales into blennies—is to remember that other creatures have come before us from faraway places, and that our infinite realm must have even more infinity along its edges.

Existence extends through space, as it does through time.

We are a sea in a solar system of seas.

What do we know of life? The alchemy of the ocean provides our essence. We take its oxygen and calcium, its plankton and its meat, and we turn it into frenetic, multiplying life. We take its roiling energy, too. We know that all creatures need food and water and a place to live. But what about empathy and love? We have grown too advanced and complicated to prosper without a purpose.

Can love be a purpose?

Or is it what we substitute for the absence of one?

Some say God is the jellyfish, the very essence of water jolted alive, but personally I think that idea is stupid.

God is the absence of everything else. A purpose.

When I was younger, one of a thousand before I became one of six, I marveled at the clearer water, at how it shimmered along its upper reaches, sparkling beneath the last glimmering rays of sun, and then how it darkened as it deepened—colors filtering out one by one, even as the particles and protozoa multiplied and the water became thick.

When food floats down to the ocean's floor, the life processes there are so slowed that it takes nearly forever for the food to rot. We think of it as manna. We are grateful for it, but it is expected. There is always something sinking down—onto a ledge or crag, or into your mouth. Some say the heaps of dead creatures across the substrate must be a sign of God—proof of his existence, an indication of his love. It's food you don't have to kill for, that arrives as benefaction. Isn't that the sign of a blessed life?

But seeing a hundred of our kind gorging on the ocean floor, tearing bodies apart with their teeth, does not fill me with a good kind of belief.

We live. We die. Some of us love.

Everything else is distraction.

We number in the millions, or the billions. There is no way to count. Like particles of water, none of us stays in the same place very long. Sometimes we'll sweep along the continental slopes or above the mid-ocean ridges, seamounts, and abyssal hills, stealing through the twilight and midnight zones, invisible to anyone who relies on their eyes to see. But mostly we remain at four and five hundred fathoms, where the intelligent animals all know who and what we are. Even the sea cucumber, who breathes through its anus, clad in that frolicsome ring of teeth.

We have no need to spurt murky clouds of ink or mucus, or trail tentacles barbed with nematocysts behind us. There are two ways to catch your prey: bite down with crushing, edged, or serrated teeth, or open your mouth so quickly it creates a vacuum and your victim is sucked inside. You can also emit loud bangs to stun them, and sometimes this makes the smaller fish hemorrhage inside. If you do it right, your prey transforms into a delicious stew. Some of us will then take a stunned, scrambled fish to the volcanic vents to turn it into a savory meat pocket. But like other creatures, we enjoy variation in our diet. Gulps of plankton are quick and easy, but algae, bacteria, and protozoa three times a day is a recipe for monotonous meals.

We hunt by day, because that is the proper thing to do. To kill at night is disgraceful.

When you gave in to my advances, I thought I was the luckiest creature in the ocean. You laughed when my belly turned bright scarlet. I couldn't hide it. You knew I was aroused. Like other males, I'd spent my youth watching female shrimp molt—who wouldn't want to watch them strip in public, drop all that body armor, and become so open and defenseless? Of course, you had armor too, but that was just your good sense. I swam endless loops around you until you let me approach. I know you sniffed me each time I passed, and I peed a little so you could smell that, too.

Then I took my chance and came closer, and I saw you were drinking my effluvia. And then I drank yours, and we were heart-break, hope, misinterpretation, and wonder, and that was love.

The amazing thing about your body was when you'd inflate your chest like two pufferfish. You always knew how big to go, not like those others who just want to astonish you.

You even let your skin turn translucent for me on our first date, so I could peer inside.

2

We are peaceful and serene. That's what we like to say, since there's no one in our world to correct us. The equator does not stop our movements from hemisphere to hemisphere, as it does the whales. But that does not mean we are all brothers and sisters. Or that we are even friends. Sometimes I wonder if our cultures have grown too different, too far apart. We are shards of a single shell that have been swept away by the current, breaking and tumbling until too many pieces have been lost. Or else they've become too eroded to fit back together. There is much to argue about besides protecting territory, mates, offspring, food. You hardly need a brain for that. Our domain is vast. There is room for all of us here. There always will be room. There is space enough even for the marauding whales, even if they have their own inscrutable reasons for not using it all.

It is shameful to be that large and superstitious.

I'll say it again: it is shameful to be a sissy whale afraid of the unknown or of swimming in the dark.

Once we were a single, perfect shell. Perhaps we were a nautilus who grew within it, forever expanding in marvelous, glistening whorls.

Or maybe we were slime worms. Or squirming eels in the abyss.

We were never tuna. We were never anchovies.

Eventually, we became something important. We grew, we flourished, we scattered. We explored. The ocean made us, but we remade ourselves.

As we expect our offspring to do.

There are seven tribes now. Cousins who no longer acknowledge one another. Just like the fish.

The 'Akl'shlw'rēre, or Akla,* make their home in the Tasman Sea. When their males come of age, they rub their bodies against the sharpest rocks until their skin is as striated as scallop shells. Their females gather around them to watch and ululate and shriek, but they keep their own skin smooth and soft. Once the males' bodies are bleeding from their wounds, the females launch into a series of incessant clicks, reminiscent of the popping and crackling of snapping shrimp, meant to warn others that their males have reached

---

*No precise phonological system exists for translating the species' names into another language. The transcriptions above are approximate, and the shortened forms, meant to aid the reader, serve the additional purpose of eliminating lexicographic errors. The names of the seven tribes are alphabetized according to their closest matches in ISO basic Latin. As with many languages, declensions denote case and number, as well as the hierarchy and gender of the speaker and listener. Nevertheless, all words are actually verbs. Additional inflections and intonations, whether for the auditory benefit of listeners or as possible relics of older grammatical forms, are dependent on variations in ocean chemistry, temperature, depth (likely gauged by ambient pressure or its mechanical effects on the species' vocal apparatus), and the distance between two or more speakers, such that positional inflections may be required at multiple times during a single conversation. This provides a rough GPS signature to each utterance that can, in turn, be embedded into memorized song. The fracturing of the seven tribes from a single historical group into ones with distinct dialects has led each to use its name as the correct term for the entire species and language. However, an umbrella term, although rarely used, does exist in all dialects: *yc*.

adulthood and are now prepared to fight. The sharks know this is not a good time to satisfy their bloodlust. A few adolescents invariably attack, and the Akla reprisal is always brutal.

Once their markings have been completed in the grisly rite, the Akla males never add to them later in life.

The Banj'xhōlla, or Banjxa, once kept to the north, but now they race up and down the sunken coasts. They are renowned as swimmers: fast and strong, and also cunning. They employ a particular flick of their caudal fin, which is hard to replicate and can easily launch swimmers off course, depending on the particular way they do it wrong. (Some of us have tried to learn by watching them from behind lava tubes, and I've seen unlucky friends careen into sheer walls at unlikely angles as a result.) But when the maneuver is performed precisely, the Banjxa can arrive and disappear like water from a fissure, with nearly the same telltale hiss. The Banjxa do not eat cephalopods because of an ancient legend regarding our origins, but they're very fond of snails and slugs, which they ridicule for their lack of speed. Occasionally, the Banjxa will hold snail-eating contests, which can only be regarded as a show of hubris. It's just bad taste.

Their legend states that a primitive, gargantuan ur-octopus allowed its tentacles to detach from its body and that each of them dissolved into one of our tribes—while the eighth was lost, or sank into a chasm, or shriveled up and died, or was devoured by others, depending on the beliefs of each particular Banjxa sect. The rest of the octopus's body then became the other creatures in the ocean, including the snails and slugs, which is what happens when brain cells are sloughed and turned into mucus. Many say that swimming isn't the only thing the Banjxa do too quickly, but it is not my aim to judge.

The Ca'avaj'u'usll, or Caavaju, embrace a very different legend. They live in the South and East China Seas, areas of the sparsest population—where once the fish were as thick as swirls of sand and you only had to let them swim into your mouth. Their mythology is similarly hard to swallow, but essentially hinges on the idea that a perfect world would be imperfect if they weren't in it, and thus they see themselves as priests in the celebratory cult of their own existence. Like clownfish, wrasses, and moray eels, they will sometimes change genders if a dominant male or female disappears from their group, although this is more focused on power dynamics and occultism than sexual orientation or expression. (All our species are capable of this, but we are capable of many things we choose not to do.) Occasionally, I have heard a Caavaju will attempt to fertilize herself, so great is their self-esteem, but I am skeptical about how this would work out. And yet they consider themselves the most refined of our species, and they view the rest of us with the disdain of master teachers who believe they've watched their students squander their gifts. They echolocate with great enunciation. The Caavaju are bores.

Everyone wants to be a Dilidillil, or Dilidi. Everyone says the Dilidi have the most fun, even more than butterflyfish and parrotfish combined. The Dilidi maintain a strict interdiction about collecting shells, which they consider stealing someone else's home. They don't swim very fast. Their males mate with many females. Their females mate with many males. They view eating and sleeping as important rites. Along with singing, snacking, and evacuating their bowels. Then they convince the whales and dolphins to sing for them, while they sway and twirl and twist. The Dilidi are not from anywhere in particular, since being a Dilidi is more a state of mind. But that doesn't mean they're unaware of borders.

The Ec'dda'kl'ēz, or Ecdda, are barbaric killers. They are not warriors or hunters, like the Akla. They are beasts. We frequently see them in the company of sharks, lurking along the fringes of expanding shrouds of blood. Their greatest delicacy is another animal's tongue. And instead of devouring brains, they prefer to pull them apart like coral tubes—until their fragments float toward the surf or sink down like bits of excrement. Like the Dilidi, the Ecdda live everywhere. Too many of them together becomes a churning tide. Disgraceful creatures, they let remoras cling to their skin. The more, the better. Fearsome? Yes. But that means they have no privacy.

The Fan'tāskla, or Fantaskla, are a mystery. There's not even proof they exist. Some say they are ghosts, but that is silly.

And we are the Gjalā'niru, or Gjala. We love—and, if we lose that love, it feels like having a pufferfish inside our hearts, ricocheting and ramming into the walls. But before that loss occurs, the spines of love are like an armor facing out, and the things we feel are impregnable to anything.

The only permanent escape from loss is death.

When we met, I wanted to build a family: a thousand kids, a safe place where we could love or hide. We don't wear shells like many of the creatures you come across on a daily basis, and I've never been especially fond of sleeping in caves. I prefer a fresh current nestling around me at night, water slipping and slapping against the rocks.

What did I hope for? That we'd become each other's home, a movable fortress with nooks and crannies, where we could put our memories and keep them safe. I wanted the opposite of the ocean's endless space. But I also thought our fortress could be a boundary that would move around with us, like the wake that forms behind you when you swim and doesn't disappear until you stop.

That first time we kissed behind the corals, and we thought no one was looking, you wiggled your snout and said, "You better not turn out to be an Ecdda and eat my tongue." So I promised you I wouldn't. I knew it would be easier for you to talk if you still had it, and I expected that same propriety from you. But love and friendship are a dodgy business, and we both understood the risk of running out of things to say.

"Kiss me again. Kiss me again," you whispered.

That's always how it starts. Each of us has flavor, piquancy, texture, tang. We taste, and we're tasted. It never hurts how we appear. Or how we ripple and contort, as the water rushes past us and broadcasts our scent. But it's not just the currents that matter: a tongue has to pay its keep. Our tongues are explorers, like the rest of our bodies. Our tongues are preachers. Our tongues are minstrels. Our mouths are hunters. Our tongues are their lures and spears. Only sometimes are they sheathed inside our cheeks.

When we gnash our teeth, our tongues know to get out of the way. But when we close our lips, they're like garden eels protruding from the sand, and then they start to feast.

"Kiss me again. Taste me again."

Once everything we did was simple. We were newborns ourselves, and our offspring were only our imagination.

We didn't have to be the Ecdda to reach out and take, but neither of us knew that yet. Then as soon as there's blood in the water, everyone's suddenly interested.

3

When I found the body, I understood it as manna, too. When food sinks through the water, you don't ask why. There are creatures above us, and they can't live forever.

We don't believe you can possess areas of the ocean, but you still need to protect them. You can only own what's attached to your body and that other animals can't tear off. The rule of the ocean is finders keepers. We tell our children to stay aware.

It had slipped into a crevice, beyond where our camp's outliers normally hunt and our swimmers patrol. The place we used to visit. The twilight space where I lost you, and then you disappeared. It's the only physical reminder I have of us beyond our nest. So I keep going, I have to, even if I know it'll never be the same water twice.

"I like this place," you'd tell me. "I like the way it smells. It smells of you."

But now there was this instead.

It looked like a cross between a toadfish and a Weddell seal, with a splash of cock-eyed squid and dugong blended in. Imagine a creature with a patch of cilia on its head and a body so weak it needed clumps of algae just to hold it together.

At first it was a sorry, eerie sight—its swollen body swirling listlessly in an eddy inside the rift, with glassy eyes and its gaping mouth already a pit of cleaner shrimp. Its limbs hung down, with its hindquarters up, and its body suspended like a giant isopod ready to pounce. More cilia spread across those limbs, while algae clung to its skin like shreds of kelp, joined to itself by an array of minuscule ligaments.

But you'd never say that sturdiness applied to the rest of its body. How pitiful that shriveled mass between its legs, a shameful approximation of an anglerfish lure, although it's true you couldn't help but want to tug at it with your teeth. And what of those two misshapen glands on either side, stuffed inside that spongy sac? Only the shrimp can explain why they didn't devour those gnarled growths outright.

The sea cucumbers snickered, but everyone knows that is overcompensation.

We keep away from the surface. We swim, we glide. When we descend, the water forms a slipstream behind us, but it also envelops and embraces us, while the pressure squeezes and tapers us, and lets us swim faster. You don't have to be a Banjxa for that. We are proud of our propulsiveness. But as we ascend, and the ambient pressure drops from a hundred atmospheres to just a few, we can feel ourselves expand. You're aware of your skin going thin, as it begins to dissolve and tear, until there is nothing left to hold you together. No, we do not burst. I don't think that would be likely. But we do not dilly-dally. It is tough enough to breathe, or to talk or think. The sun will burn you, and the tiny world will penetrate your skin. So we keep our distance. We are aloof.

And also we have never cared. Why focus on the surface when the rest of the ocean, and all its wonderment and complexity, is underneath? We are used to unfathomable creatures in our unfathomable ocean and to the mangled ones that somehow still survive. What's even in the air? Poison, emptiness? Is there food? I know there are currents, but you've got to put something decent in them if you want our attention.

I nudged the body toward our camp, over the sand, rock, clay, and ooze. I didn't have to use my teeth. My snout and fins were enough to propel it. It moved awkwardly through the currents, more like a piece of elkhorn coral that had broken from its base, tumbling as much as it would glide. Other Gjala amassed and followed me. But they weren't the only ones. Envoys from each of our tribes arrived as soon as news of the creature's discovery spread.

We keep away from the coastlines and continental shelves, until they transform into the deeper slopes and rises leading to the ocean floor. None of us had ever seen a land creature before, although a few Dilidi claimed they had. But they were more like seahorses or sea slugs, the way they told it.

The calm lasted longer than any of us expected. You can race halfway across an ocean if you need to, but that doesn't explain what to do once you arrive. At first, there was quiet. Water will sometimes appear to idle and slip into repose. But that means you're trapped inside a moment. Or a bubble. Because our whole existence is founded on the idea that currents are what convey meaning, and there's no way to keep them away. They are unpreventable and inescapable. That's how it was once the first tail started pounding. And then another. And another. Until there was nothing but a hundred, and then a thousand, and then a million or a billion sweeping tails, slapping at the ground, the rocks, the water, and at one another. Then quiet became a memory. And it became a myth, because you couldn't prove it had ever existed. And then it became a kind of irony too, because the only way to convey the myth of silence was with a song. You had to sing it louder and louder to drown the others out.

We gathered in the canyon, the only area by our camp broad enough to contain us all: the envoys from each of our tribes surrounded by their swimmers, and the curious others who'd followed in their wakes. The creature's discovery was shocking for everything it was and it wasn't, for its strangeness, its newness, and how gruesome it appeared. By now, the water was swirling madly, a roiling stew like the kind that gushes up from abyssal fissures. Its pelvic mass had already been severed, but I don't want to draw more attention to that sorry barnacle. Because what amazed us all about the creature's body were those peculiar upper limbs, with their ten bony lamprey endings, and the way you could nudge them open and closed like a jellyfish bell.

"Love me, love me now," you would tell me. "I won't live forever."

There can always be someone among us who will be the first.

It won't be you. It won't be me.

We won't know that until we're dead. Until then, I will love you like there'll always be a tomorrow.

Is tomorrow when you'll want to ask for forgiveness? Because then it will be too late.

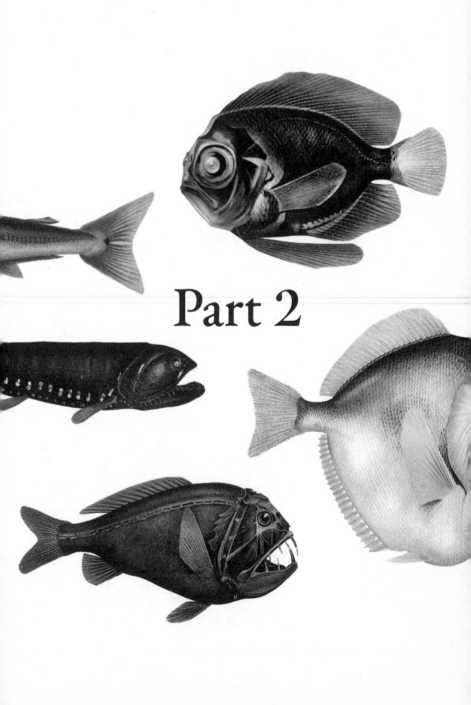

Part 2

4

Water batters everything, brutally or softly. What it leaves behind, we pummel ourselves. We don't do that softly.

I entrusted the body to Gjila,* our beloved adviser. Each of our tribes is scattered across multiple camps—our dialects and customs are so different that we can easily recognize which ones are our own—and there was no one in ours I had more faith in. Maybe Gola would give up his life for me in a fight, but Gjila was skilled enough that he wouldn't have to. I'd been careful with the creature when I found it, but by the time the envoys from the other tribes arrived, along with additional Gjala, we saw that its body had been mangled. It weighed on us that we'd permitted this to occur. Most of us suspected the Ecdda, although what they'd do with it was another question. Would you really want to feed on the lamentable organ—allowing it, with all its swollen shrunken wriggliness, to flop inside your mouth?

What if it were the only one in the entire ocean?

The only plausible explanation was that it had been swallowed. Otherwise, even our fry would have been able to find it. A limb—if you can call it that—releases a billion particles into the water when it's severed from a body, and even a single one would be effortless to

*Gjilā'anï'shl'ez.

detect. A wound communicates itself to the world, spreading news of injury, anguish, and the possibility of lunch. But were we ready to make accusations against a tribe that was probably hoping just for that? And were we prepared for what would ensue?

Gjila has many sayings: Do not start a fight unless you are prepared to maim or kill to win (killing is better, because maiming invariably leads to grudges). Do not fight for honor, since the memory of dishonor is eventually torn and tangled like a strand of kelp. Do not fight for vengeance, since vengeance leads to emptiness and remorse, making you unreliable to friends. Do not fight for mates because there will always be other fish in the sea. Fight for sport, since sport is a form of exercise. Fight for tongue, since it is a delicacy. Fight for food when you are hungry, since hunger leads to desperation and transforms you into a slow-moving target (and then more quickly into the remaining parts of one). But once you're sated, overeating is heinous, since it is brutish and disrespectful. When possible, love. When that's impossible, swim away.

Never fight about what's not important. When in doubt, ask yourself: Am I willing to die in this battle? Do not fight for causes. Only for ends.

Live your life so that you'll be missed. But never before you're gone.

Brola* of the Banjxa pressed to the front. He'd arrived to our waters first, accompanied by his fastest swimmers, with more Banjxa in their wake. Even now, they swooped past the rest of us, adding to the confusion as they filled the water column with foam and fins,

---

*Brol'āyi'kī'usl.

tails and sand. As I've said, we are a tranquil species, given to subtle and deliberate movements. So a thousand Banjxa propelling themselves at breakneck speeds was an opening gambit. Chop and awe.

Brola offered introductory comments as soon as we could make him out again. First, he stuck to the facts: the creature had been discovered, we didn't know where it came from or how it got here, and news of it had spread through our various seas. That's to say he started with the obvious. Or what we generally call science. But even in the mayhem, we could see the Ecdda sniggering, gills opening and closing contemptuously. Then Brola flicked his tail triumphantly and continued to address the amorphous, still-multiplying pack:

"Once we were a single creature. Salt and sand and currents shaped us, once we split from a common whole. You may not believe we came from Ooo,[*] the great octopus, who gave birth to us all. Some say the ocean formed us in one dark gushing corner of an abyssal cave, although that requires healthy amounts of imagination, and more of it than I have myself. For like many of you, I only believe what I know is true. But those are the stories we sing, when we aren't focused on what's pressed against our teeth. Perhaps we weren't the first ones inside the cave, just as we weren't Ooo's only arm. But we can all agree that this pitiful creature that brings us together didn't emerge from the same place as the rest of us here. And I won't try to fool you by saying that it is one of our lost tribes—the silly one that drifted too far away.

"Today, I call you 'cousins.' I don't call you brothers. I have a thousand brothers, and most of them are not you. It's been this way for as long as any of us can remember. We've drifted away from one another. But I know this animal wrapped in algae is not my brother

---

[*]O'o'ō'xla'hōlla.

or my cousin, and that isn't an exaggeration—you can see and smell and taste that it's the truth. So perhaps we're here because it's time for us to come back together, and go back to being one school. Isn't that why this creature's important? Isn't that why it matters? Once, we were all brothers and sisters. Once, we were all the same thing."

It was a moving speech, but pure guppy shit. Only the parrot-fish, who sometimes understand a few of our words and phrases, would be convinced.

Clova* of the Caavaju spoke next. The Banjxa never stopped flitting through the water, even once Brola returned to their ranks.

"Maybe this creature's arrival means there are others in the world to hear our stories," Clova began. "Maybe this creature and its kind are intelligent—there's obviously more to it than a slug—and they'll recognize the intelligence and poetry in our stories, too. Maybe this creature was even an explorer, who came to our world to learn about who we are, although you'd think everyone would already know that. But wherever it's from, we can guess it's not as appealing as it is here. Perhaps this sorry figure even died from seeing our world's beauty. That itself is a beautiful thought."

Clova paused to let his words seep through the water. Then he added, "This creature has done us a service for letting us think that together. How fortunate we are to have it here, for all the things we can learn from it about us."

---

*Clo'vā'shlw'rēle.

5

The Ecdda licked their lips. The Dilidi didn't need to speak. The Fantaskla stayed along the outskirts, if they were there at all.

I could feel the currents at my back, pushing me before the throng. I'd been the one to find the body. I don't know if that made me an expert, but they were in our camp, and that made it my turn now:

"Yes, we call each other 'cousin.' That's always been our term of affection. True, cousins sometimes kill each other, but they usually do it less than brothers. Still, I've always hoped the word 'cousin' could remind us what was possible. Not turn us into obedient and orderly schools, like Brola of the Banjxa says. But as a way of acknowledging our single beginning and common ends. Maybe that can give meaning to the vast middle sea, which is where all of us live.

"But now this creature has our attention. We know of millions of forms of life. The ones we barely notice, and others we don't see anymore. But now there's something new. A body here, and it isn't like ours. It isn't like anyone's. You might think it's gruesome, with its pasty skin and grassy splotches. Or you might think it's delectable—with strange bits and pieces beyond its tongue that you can't resist stuffing inside your mouth, even if this is the first time one like it was ever found and there might have been a point to keeping it intact. But surely this animal is not the only of its kind. There may be thousands like it, or even more. But this one sank to us. It came to us, it gave itself. And that made it ours. Obviously, it's unsuited for love, or those parts wouldn't have been so easy to remove. But maybe it has something else worthwhile."

"I'm sure that's what it believed," Clova observed. "Many creatures think highly of themselves, for no good reason."

At this point, Gola seemed about to speak. But then he started floating up.

Currents pound. Eddies swirl. Storms sweep across the plains, devastating anything in their paths. Fissures open. Sediment roils. Hydrothermal vents spew sulfides and sulfates into water columns, transforming basalt into gnarled lava pillars twice the length of whales. Then those crack and break, and turn into crushing rain. You find crabs and shrimp pulverized by their remains. What use are shells against that kind of onslaught? These things happen. Catastrophes happen. Heartbreak happens—and it almost feels the same. But what doesn't happen is a giant creature, nearly the same size as us, showing up in our world, with cuttlefish beaks on its claws. And I don't mean it happens rarely. Because it happens never.

Once life in the ocean was simpler. Once there weren't questions. We all looked and thought alike, and the water stayed the same and provided the same life. Sure, there were subtle differences in our features and smells. But was there enough differentiation to feel the crush of another's desires and doubts against your own? No, there was sameness, and sameness is comfortable, like a balmy current. Once it's gone, you feel its absence. And the chill.

That comfort was something we couldn't get enough of. Everyone always wants more. But then questions came in a trickle. What existed before us? What comes next? The endless whats and ifs and whys.

We have memories and stories. We have songs. But how many of those can you keep inside your head?

This creature is a question, too. Worse, it's a question that eats and breathes. Or I assume it used to. It got here out of narcissism, generosity, animosity, or a mistake.

Once it probably did a lot of things. Or do you think it spent its days fixed in one place, barely moving like a conch?

Do questions like these push the sureness and uncertainty of love away—and stir our world until neither of them can exist? The ocean isn't patient. It is persistent.

We live in a world of sharks and storms. Despite its grandeur and beauty, it's never going to be safe here, truly. We know this from the start.

It used to be fun to pretend. We'd nuzzle together in caves and imagine the rest of the world wasn't outside, not the broken shells or hyperiid amphipods or giant squids or the nosy fish. I'd try to imagine an invisible force field, a flawlessly transparent sheet of ice. You could see and smell and hear through it—you'd bump your head if you swam into it—but we'd be safe inside.

Then the walls of our cave would recede. All we'd have to do was use our minds to move them back, and the creaking stones would make more room, creating a succession of spaces and chambers, like the inside of a heart. This would be our world, a place where we could stay, untouched, forever. The real world is home to many creatures, but a universe is only two.

We'd remain untouched, while we touched each other. We would be all we'd need.

6

When I was young, I was easily impressed. The ocean is full of the strangest creatures. There's no way to see it but like that.

Some flatworms duel with their penises to decide which one should be female. The winner injects the loser with its sperm.

Blind, jawless hagfish release clouds of mucus to deter predators, or possibly to suffocate them. But amphipods consider that mucus the finest delicacy.

You can undulate or flick your fins to move. Or you can shoot water from your anus, for jet propulsion. It's one thing to do it, but quite another to want to be observed in the act.

Perhaps a jellyfish is nothing more than a writhing bladder.

Vampire squids turn themselves inside out.

The puny male anglerfish latches on to the larger female. Then his body atrophies and fuses with her until all that remains are a pair of gonads jutting out of her flank, providing sperm on demand when she's ready to spawn.

The Pacific viperfish's teeth are so long it can't ever close its mouth.

Redfin batfish walk like lobsters.

The male thornback cowfish emits a high-pitched hum during mating, which somehow the females don't find distracting.

Cod swim along the ocean's bottom, gulping and swallowing clams whole. They digest what's inside, and then stack the shells inside their stomachs, like little towers.

The blobfish are exactly that.

And then there are creatures, like the salmonids, who abandon the salt of the ocean to find soft waters to spawn and die in. They die and dissolve. Their bodies turn into nitrogen and protein, and their children digest them. Maybe they're not the most attentive parents, but isn't that also commitment? Fish of my fish. Flesh of my flesh.

Long ago, we set out to explore and conquer other seas. The creatures there didn't know what to make of us. And they didn't know how to resist. We bent many of them to our will. We banished others. A few we may have decimated, so delectable were their stocks.

Maybe the Caavaju are right. We were convinced the ocean was perfect because we were in it. The more of us there were, the better it was for everyone—for all the ocean life. And the more places we settled, the better still. That should have been obvious.

7

The creature's appendages were what fascinated us most.

Not the scraps of lettuce coral on the sides of its head. Not the nostrilled protuberance in the center of its face, lacking all the cohesiveness of a well-formed snout. Not the jack-thick hind limbs that could have only moved it forward at the pace of a slug. And definitely not the pendulous urchins clinging to the sides of its disgraced pelvis.

I mean the spindly, sickly, flabby set on top—the ones astride its chest, on either side of its heart. There had to be something special about how the blood in the creature's body powered those feeble limbs. You could imagine it waving them like a pair of antennae. What use could they possibly have, when you could easily snap the jointed parts between your teeth? They dangled from the creature's sides like strands of kelp, each as fluttery as the dorsal fin on a Moorish idol. Its neck wasn't much thicker than its upper limbs, and its head got stuck inside a cranny when we flopped it over. Some thought the easiest thing would just be to pull it off, but we all saw how it might get lost. Especially in a current. Or to our rapscallion fry, who'd want it for a game.

Still, those feeble limbs were what held our attention, the way the minute appendages at their ends closed as pincers or opened as severed fins, all together or one at a time. In any combination.

Beside them, the head couldn't compare. It didn't look capable of much.

Bristleworms, flounders, lobsters, crabs, anemones, eels: they live on the ocean floor. The intricacies of our world go on above them. Every once in a while, we'll see an ariid catfish, despicable creatures. The way they comb through the sand for bits of the dead tells you all you really need to know.

The first thing we urge our young once they're physically able is: swim up. The world happens all around you, in every direction. The world is high. The world is deep. But it expands in front of your eyes and nares, so that you can always return to where you started if you just keep going straight.

The salmon know this. That's what makes them delicious.

They swim into the open seas. Some of them turn around to retrace their flicks, but others keep going until they're back where they began. They see things that amaze them on the way.

Sometimes our young don't want to explore, but how else can they gain perspective? We nudge them into open water. Most of them return. Then they become more delicious to one another, too. That's the value of encountering wondrous things.

The first time I saw a deep-sea trench sundering the floor beneath me, I realized how minuscule we were. The bathypelagic world belongs at a distance. The hadal zone is no joke. Going there means a lot of pressure.

But once I reached it after hours of swimming, I realized I still wasn't as big as I thought. The nether reaches of my body disappeared into the abysmal murk. I was only a face, with my tongue lost inside my mouth. The creatures at these depths survive on the planet's internal heat. Many of them don't have faces at all, so I've always felt we had an advantage. But I knew I'd have to return home to be myself. It's the strangest world I've ever experienced, and it's not like you can invite the creatures you meet there to come and visit.

Once I was back in our Gjala seas, I thought nothing else would surprise me. I had a face with eyes, but I lacked perspective. You could do a lot with appendages like the creature had. Calling them pincers seemed inapt. Maybe a better choice was "clingers." The nubby ones at the ends of its legs must have served some vestigial purpose, when its world possessed more for it to hold, but the crowd on the forelimbs was another story.

And "story" is exactly the word I mean, because we debated what those appendages were for. Had the creature been alive, the easiest thing would have been to ask. I can't say it looked especially intelligent, but you would reasonably expect it to know. (Crabs and shrimp aren't that bright either. Creatures with pincers rarely are.)

Did I say there were ten? Maybe there were even twenty.

Then Gjila said, "Can we even be sure it could talk?" and that also was a reasonable question.

But Brola of the Banjxa, scourge of these welcoming seas, had his own ideas about the bendy, spindly clingers. Nudging their tips with his snout, he showed how they could curl together, until they formed the shape of a sea cucumber's toothy anus.

Our juveniles saw this, and they sniggered.

Open, closed, open, closed. Now you see it, now you don't.

It was an amusing trick. Then Brola approached the aperture with his lips and let his tongue play about it as well. The Banjxa move so quickly that there's never a warning when they're going to do something revolting.

As he pulled his mouth away, he unloosed a stream of bubbles. Then he took the listless limb in his teeth and drove it, curled clingers first, into the ground. He was careful not to jerk it from the upper joint, so that the limb remained attached to the rest of the body. The clump made a hole in the sand, with a speed and breadth any burrowing creature would have to envy. Then Brola withdrew it and made another. And another.

And another—punching at the sand with just one of the limbs, before he incorporated the second one as well. Until there was a patchwork of crevices spread out before us, a battery of undulations and cavities in the ground.

To see a thresher shark slap its tail at a school of mackerel is to witness a similar kind of brutality and carnage. A few lucky fish are hurled away, but most are stunned. Some are maimed. Their lifeless bodies are swallowed one by one, with a savagery that turns the thresher sharks' feeding into a game. Is it better to die when you're unconscious, or to have the chance to stare your predator in the eye?

The threshers whip their tails like strands of kelp, but they do it with the force of whales. One snap is usually enough. But sometimes they'll repeat it, and then you hear the percussive beat of violence all around you. If you aren't careful, you can forget to be alarmed.

8

I grew up in broiling seas that smelled of magnesium carbonate freckled with desire. A spewing vent outside a cave marked the place a thousand of us called home (one thousand and two, counting our doting parents). One thousand and three, counting our guardian, Gola.

Back in those days, he was lithe and quick. He wasn't a Banjxa. By that I mean you could trust him. But he could dart from one sponge to another, with a reef rat or two tucked beneath his fin, without skipping the swish of his tail.

And so it broke his heart to see us get picked off one by one, swallowed, chewed, crushed, swept away, torn by gnashing teeth, bitten in half, poisoned, impaled. The consolidation of a family is inevitable and terrible. As much as I try, there are certain creatures I will always hate.

It isn't bias if you have good reasons. There must be creatures who don't like us, either. Perhaps they'd say they have good reasons, too.

Are all my lost brothers and sisters swimming together in some happy afterlife? That idea isn't crazier than any other aspect of existence.

And yet I don't believe it.

I believe we're born, we're here, and we have a single chance. Some of those chances last as long as a tide. Some, only as long as it takes a jaw to clamp shut. Some last more than a generation. But there's no thing as a second chance. There is only one chance, because nothing stops and starts anew. The ocean is continuation.

It was a happy place, our vent, our sea, our home. Diminishing numbers of siblings, true, but there were always still so many of us around. We played! Gola, too! We'd hide. He'd swim, and look for us. And also true, some of us never showed up at the end. That added an element of unpredictability to the game.

Our parents seemed resigned but content. They'd come back with food from hunting expeditions. With fewer mouths in their brood each time, there was always enough. We feasted! We ate until we thought we were going to burst. (It was your own fault if you did.) I remember one time they came home with shrimp, scrambling masses of them, and we marched them toward the vent and popped them into our mouths as soon as they were freshly sizzled.

Yes, shrimp don't like us much—but I've already said what I had to about creatures with pincers.

Gola could gobble an army of them up. Once the rest of us had finished, we'd watch him keep going, shoveling the shrimp past his snout, swallowing even as he'd start to laugh, and then all of us would laugh along with him. Hundreds of us laughing, yes, that's a happy meal.

Supposedly there are creatures that stop eating once they've had enough, but cultivated ones know to keep eating for just a bit longer, so they can concentrate on the flavor and the mouthfeel without the distraction of hunger getting in the way. Sizzling shrimp clawing at your palate, parboiled inside their shells!

I had an idyllic youth.

I swam, sniffed, fed, and was educated. I learned about our world. I learned that not all of us agree about so many things—some of which probably don't even exist—that the ones we agree on still can't keep us together, even if they're floating right before our eyes.

I learned that two creatures who look the same can still be so different that the only thing that unites them is mistrust.

Gola once told me, "We're all variations. That means we're all imperfect." Despite what the Caavaju say.

Every culture is a battle between competing versions of itself, half-formed customs and beliefs vying to be the only one, continually transforming to become more powerful and irresistible, while still maintaining that every previous version was also right.

Every culture is a wave, growing, surging, steepening, and approaching its inevitable crest. As long as land stays out of the way, those waves can keep getting bigger. The amount of energy in a wave is proportional to the number of molecules trapped inside it.

Ask the diatoms about the force of the water: it's almost impossible to break free.

As if you'd ever want to.

9

Gjila says, "When waging war, first send in your soldiers who can regrow their missing limbs. Next, send the ones whose limbs don't matter. Last, send the ones without any limbs at all, for only they can move as fluidly as the water."

Only they can dissolve into the currents and be everywhere in an instant.

Gjila says, "When preparing for battle, never rely on soldiers without faces, because you can't really trust them. Make peace with your loved ones. Make peace with yourself."

"Don't send in your soldiers with ruptured swim bladders," Gola adds.

"We all have ruptured swim bladders, in one way or another," Gjila says. "Life is sinking and soaring when we least expect it."

Brola kept making holes in the sand. The expanse of pocked terrain doubled in size. Groups of Akla, Banjxa, and Ecdda lingered along the edges. Yes, I insist, we are serene. If this was violence, it was only violence to the ground. But even the sea cucumbers knew to get out of the way. You always want to avoid a punch to your anus.

"When making war, there can only be one leader. When making peace, there are many. That's because peace is more complicated than war."

And what about love? I knew you grew up in roiling seas, just as I did. Three oceans away. But what is distance compared to taste and scent and chemistry? Currents take you where they want to go. The choice is to enter them, or to stay out of the way.

It's not as if they come as a surprise. The only surprise is what you find at their ends, where they taper off until they're just idyllic tremors. You found me.

Or, as you put it, "*You* found me."

No, I smelled you coming, so I had time to prepare.

And I tasted you, too. You couldn't stop me.

When we finally met, you emerged from the current as foam. And then as skin. And then as muscle and movement—liquid flits and undulations that announced your presence as adamantly as the submarining of a whale. You were flesh. You were a song. You were hydroelectric, magnetic, radiant, infrasonic.

All I had to do was let you enter me then.

I opened my skin, my gills, my mouth. I opened the parts of me that can't ever recover, no matter how much time there is to heal.

You were a chemical explosion inside my body. You were moaning without solid form. You were potential energy, catabolism, plate tectonics.

You *were* the current, and then you were *here*.

There wasn't a single word left for us to say before the first one was uttered, but both of us stuttered nervously. Then the next day was the spawn.

10

We hovered side by side, as the corals opened. A billion polyps all around us. A billion bodies opening themselves and steaming into the hot slushiness of the night.

Neither one of us dared to blink. But I breathed you.

And I saw you opening and closing your mouth, also letting parts of me in.

Some corals are male. Some are female. Some are both. But all choose the same night each year to release themselves into the clouding water. They ooze. They spew. And spurt. They expose their deepest cores and let eggs and sperm and, sometimes, bundles of them both come hurtling out.

So many of us pursue the depths, for the reassuring embrace of the ocean. But the coral let their progeny float up, where they'll meet and mate and then tumble away to grow and secrete new homes. It is creation myth, without an ounce of invention. The sea becomes a whirl of genetic goo.

It is effervescence, coralline cataclysm, frenzied abundance. A spattering hot mess, and the origin of all life. Gametes swirling toward one another in a flurry of chance and desire. And then all it takes is for two of them to touch for life suddenly, and then miraculously, and then expectedly and inevitably, to begin. It is chaotic certainty, arriving, coming, as a splash.

And so we watched the world having sex all around us, the universe expanding, sprawling, and then returning to itself as a haze of a billion particles of a thousand species finding their singular and astonishingly perfect mates. It was happening in every direction, as far as either of us could see.

We'd only just met ourselves, but what other future was there for us after this? What else but to melt into each other's breast and skin, and feel the same kinetic blood streaming through us both?

You were my salt. I was your water.

Our hearts darted around our bodies, unable to stay in any place for more than a few seconds.

We existed at six different fathoms. All at once.

I'd like to think the corals also noticed. But they were distracted. We were distracted.

In our world, this is how we begin.

We danced, our bodies intertwining. We kissed, our tongues a pair of tentacles tying knots. Our teeth, rows and rows, and now *rows* and *rows*—together, we'd be invincible! Our chests, one chest. Our nether regions, one as well. Throbbing like jellyfish and gently glowing. Radiant, with a seismic tantrum in our breasts.

Every part of me was shreds. Every part of you was shreds. Every part that was us both was raw swollen flesh.

When the spawn occurs, it is synchronous across the reefs. It doesn't matter your species, gender, or location. You sense it first as an upwelling, an impatient urge to expose every single part of yourself, from each mitochondrial split to every amoebic bulge. As the moment nears, that longing and necessity grow. You feel yourself begin to shudder. When solitary members of our kind come to watch the spawn, there is a sad exuberance at seeing this much euphoria, this much shaking and milky effluence, without being able to join in yourself.

Yes, there's some self-stimulation. But that's never the same thing.

Would we have fallen for each other, so head over tails, if we hadn't met on this particular day? Would we have continued for so long afterward if the corals hadn't been in the midst of their rapture? Would our world still be lost in that reverie we called peace? Would you still be alive?

We spawn, the corals spawn, we watch them exude calcium carbonate where they land, creating structure. We watch them build, constructing cities, secreting new reefs over thousands of years, so slowly that their method is a secret. The secret is having patience.

They're nearly gone now, too.

11

Brola kept pounding, breaking any bits of coral, flattening fragments in the sand. Gola shivered and started floating up, but I think he was doing it on purpose. He flicked his tail and started to swim, as fast as he could.

Eat, and don't get eaten. Break, and don't get broken.

When there's no other option, *flee.*

By now, the creature had started drifting apart. Soft filmy skin had turned to sponge. The outer layers were tattered, while hints of bones shone through. At a basic level, beneath our skin and flesh, we're all made of coral reef: a lattice of gnarled calcium, with blood vessels and nerves poking through.

This coral lacked our world's vibrant color.

I wonder how long it took this creature to build its skeleton.

I wonder if it was sad.

Of course, Brola and the Banjxa didn't care about that. Nor the Akla or the Ecdda. When the Banjxa swim and dart, there's no time to think. That's how it was for them now. I could imagine Gola treading away clumsily, weighed down by his thoughts.

His absence wouldn't be noticed. Except by me.

The thing about holes is they always fill. There are no empty spaces in the ocean, no vacuums. Water sweeps in sand and nearby shells. So you have to keep digging, finning, and pounding. It's a losing battle, like swimming into a relentless current. Eventually you tire, while the ocean doesn't even notice.

The water doesn't know who or what is in it.

Gjila says, "If you're going to fight, make sure it's against another living creature. Otherwise, there's no possible outcome but for you to lose."

Or even better: choose an opponent who's already dead. Maybe like the one we'd found. The Banjxa always like to present themselves as victors.

Gjila says, "When digging holes, you can create channels in the silt by shooting water from your anus while others hold you down. But try to avoid it."

Gjila says, "When digging holes, it's true that if you bend those clingers together into a point, they work like the end of a cuttlefish beak. But you can also use them individually to form patterns in the sand."

We watched him tug the limb from Brola's mouth, the rest of the body still attached and twisting awkwardly in the current. Brola was amazed by Gjila's fearlessness or daring. I'm not sure any of us knew which one it was. But then he let the limb go, not even showing his teeth. Gjila dragged it across the grains, until he'd drawn the rough outline of a gorgonian in the sand.

Then the current came, as it always does.

12

We live in open spaces. They extend in all directions, including the vastness of up and down, and when any of us needs more room, those spaces can just become larger. We do not crowd.

You do not tread on someone else's fins.

The coral reefs live by other rules. They live in cities, one on top of another, in a kind of abominable symbiosis that makes it impossible to be alone.

The algae insinuate themselves inside the corals. (I would not like anyone to insinuate himself into me.) They produce food from light and surrender most of it to their lazy hosts. Yes, the corals are lazy, except for once a year when they're invigorated by having sex. But the reefs are part of a larger scheme of interdependence, where every creature has three roles: to live, to breed, and to provide for the others in their community. When creatures die, they become food. When snails die, their vacant shells become new homes as well. The algae use the coral waste as fertilizer, which helps them grow. Worms and sea cucumbers then forage the reef, scrubbing it clean. Clams and sea squirts filter water, extracting food and expelling water that you can taste is purer. Shrimp and gobies rid turtles and other fish of parasites, pecking them off their skin and the insides of their mouths and gills— tending to hundreds in a day. Some hermit crabs place sponges on their shells, where the sponges can grow free from predators. As those sponges grow, they camouflage the crabs, while the toxins in their cells protect the crabs from any who might want to eat them. Small jacks swim next to larger queen triggerfish, hidden by their trunks until it's time to surprise their quarry, which they attack together and share. Even large predator species, like sharks and groupers, manage the reef community, making sure there isn't an imbalance in the population. It's true, sharks have a role, as much as I hate to admit it.

And we? Sometimes we're eaten while we're alive, but mostly we just think about ourselves.

The coral cities expand. We watch them cover mounts and stones. We watch them sprawl. We watch them die.

Cities turn white, and then they crumble and dissolve. Once they were an empire. Once they were something more to behold.

And still the corals insist on building their cities, perhaps because the creatures living inside them wouldn't survive anywhere else. So it is an act of determination. And of grace.

Grace doesn't require you to be able to swim. Gola is the most graceful being I know. Wherever he is now.

We sprawl in a different way. In a way that says that all we see in the world is ours. And that we will exist here forever.

We will grow larger and larger, as species do, until we are larger than the whales. And there will always be room for us. The Dilidi say we should not allow ourselves to be caught in an interdependent relationship with other creatures, because if one of them suffers, then we'll all be affected. They ask, Isn't that our right, to swim alone?

What does the group consciousness of the corals get you? The convenience of sharing your mortality? The corals were supposed to live forever.

The world is one cosmic ocean inside a galaxy of oceans, stretching out into the watery unknown. Cities won't exist in the future, because they exist in finite time and space. The only future is to expand, to go new places, to explore. There are still places in this world we don't know. Just look at this creature, even if he's already disintegrating, and dissolving, too. If you look at how weak he seems, you can guess he depended on others.

13

I did my best to trace the form of a gorgonian, too. At first I tried with the edge of my tail, and then with one fin, but I didn't have the proper angle. I'd wait until there was a lull in the current, but my shapes would disappear . . . before they'd fully taken shape.

I kept thinking of Gjila's etching and how suddenly there was a sea fan in the sand. It wasn't a fan, but what else would you call it? Then it was gone. You risk everything the moment you look away.

You see things, sometimes. Suddenly there's the outline of a crab in leaf coral, a school of sardines in the swishing of a fan, the arc of whale ribs rising from the floor of our canyon. It doesn't mean they are there. Still, they *are*. If I tell you what I've seen, you don't say I am crazy. Maybe you say you can see it too, if you cock your head and look at it just right. I suppose you could even navigate that way, using the spot where we both think it looks like there's a barracuda to mark your destination, if there weren't so many better ways to get around the ocean. Crazy is in the eye of the beholder.

There is beauty. And then there is art. We've all seen the way horse-eye jacks swirl off a coral wall, or how the salema form shoals so thick they could be walls themselves. It is pretty to watch them swim like that. But we know they'd do it anyway, if we weren't there—and they'd do it the same way if we found it ugly, and even if they *knew* we found it ugly. (I hate to belabor the point, but is there anything artful about how a sea cucumber drags itself across the sand, ingesting the world through its anus? Or maybe there is, because it makes our water purer.)

Is making a picture in the sand also art? What about the moans of whales? What about the ways the Banjxa flip through the currents? What about the markings on the Akla's skin? What about how you once let a school of anchovies swim about your neck as raiment?

Yes, I liked that. I won't forget.

What about your thoughts—mine, yours, or anyone's? Ideas that aren't about anything particular—not about food or mates or tending to our young. Thoughts that are about nothing more than how the electrons in the current taste, or how the light speckles the water at its slushing fringes, and how the way that looks is pretty.

And what about ugliness? Creative ugliness, like how you can gore the side of a spotfin butterflyfish and pin it to a rock as you watch parasites swim inside it? And the way it struggles, wrenching, when you let it paddle away. Would that be art, too?

You can take a shell or a hard-edged stone, hold it in your mouth, and scrape the outer edge against the moving sand to form a shape, and it works better than using just your fin or tail. You don't have to make a gorgonian or even any kind of coral.

It may be possible to draw a turtle.

Gjila is still the best there is. Maybe it's a matter of practice, but I don't think you need to be the first. The Banjxa have many talented swimmers. I believe they're only getting faster. Maybe the skill to make images is innate. Or maybe it takes skill, plus enthusiasm, effort, practice, and the ingenuity to devise some useful techniques. Or it has to do with the sand. If that's where the images are, they could have been there all along. Then art is being a detective. It's seeing them before they're there, and still seeing them once the currents have flushed them away. Then you could draw those images twice.

I bet you would have been good at this. I know you would have loved it.

It makes me think of you when I try to make my own. Imagine if I could draw your face. I wouldn't blink.

I'd draw you over and over. Each time you'd be different, but each time you'd be the same.

Maybe I can draw Gola. The problem is everyone always looks the same. They look like shapeless beds of giant clams. And once you used to balance oysters on your chest!

The water washes everything away, except what you keep inside yourself. But the water washes things to you, too. It washed us this creature.

Is art chance? Is water art?

Maybe Gjila is good at making pictures because he uses the creature's limb, with those separate gnarled ends. You can't hold that many shells in your mouth. They'd drop like teeth. Those clingers don't look like they'd grow back.

His gonads didn't, but he was already dead.

Besides, the idea wasn't to move them together. A sea fan's tentacles don't move as a block, but flex with the current, catching particles in their path. That's how Gjila moved the creature's limb in the sand, bending the ends individually at each possible joint, always aware of the right angles.

14

So what about pretending? Is pretending art? Pretending that you like an admirer. Or pretending you are dead.

That's popular here when some predators attack.

Most creatures you meet can't control their faces—if they're fortunate to have faces at all—except to open or close their mouths or barely to redirect their eyes. You talk to them, and their looks are glassy. The expression on the pinned butterflyfish's face, while parasites devour its intestines, is exactly the same as a rock beauty's while it's spawning. If you ask, they'll say they feel pain and ecstasy— *yes*. But their avowals are unconvincing.

And don't get me started about dolphins, with their fake, sarcastic smiles. Happy or sad, they always look the same. Smug motherfuckers.

Some species mimic others, in order to attack or as a form of defense. The bluestriped fangblenny is a combtooth blenny that more closely resembles a bluestreak cleaner wrasse. But instead of pecking off parasites, it bites into the fins of its easily duped victims. Only a fool doesn't sniff around first. The mimic octopus can disguise itself as a lionfish, sea snake, jellyfish, or speckled sole, depending on its needs. The black-marble jawfish can then disguise itself as a mimic octopus, which lets it move around safely, which is what *it* needs. The scorpionfish and stonefish just sit in place and look like schmutz.

But none of that is really pretending. It's just doing what's instinctive.

And then there are those butterflies, with their fake googly eyes on their flanks. That doesn't keep them from getting pinned to rocks.

But we are different. Our snouts and cheeks and eye sockets move unimpeded, and you'd never mistake us for anything but what we are. We make expressions. We pretend. We display. And we make it clear how we feel, even if that's not how we feel at all.

Like sharks, we are able to close our eyes. We do it for self-protection. But it's less to shield them from contact when we strike and more to block out what we don't want to see. Other fish, with their lidless eyes, don't have a choice. That must make it hard for them to dream.

We grimace, smirk, give lecherous stares. Yes, I know the Weddell seals twitch their whiskers, but we still haven't figured out what that means.

We cajole. Words play only a part in that.

This creature's face is loose and spongy. You can twist the parts around. You can tweak the protuberance, flare the nostrils, yank on the tongue and see it once was a meaty organ—capable of swelling, probing, and curling. The creature's cheeks could puff; the growths above its eyes could rise. If you tugged on them, you could then make them rise some more, until they arched like the legs of a subordinate lobster cowering before a dominant male. There are coralline sponges on the sides of its head, with more cilia inside, that might have been lures or rudimentary places for their mothers to grab them. The jaw moves independently, in an unhinged circle, while the mouth shuttles from side to side, dragging the protuberance along with it, as bait.

In short, I think this creature could also pretend. It can also close its eyes. But I doubt it had the intelligence to leer.

15

The creature comes from land. A shriveled creature, from the shriveled world. No matter how many oils their skins secrete, they must always be dirty.

They must stink.

We see birds sometimes when we approach the surface. We see them dive down to catch the fish in our realm. Being able to fly is an act of grace, a miracle, the stuff of religion. Being able to walk on land like a sea robin or frogfish isn't as impressive. There are birds that will fly nearly as far as the whales will swim. That is how much they love the water.

The creatures who live on land must crave this place where we live. They must come here to refresh, replenish. They must ache for it. They must dream it.

So far from the ocean's depths, these land-dwellers must be heavy drinkers. There must be an absence inside them they need to fill. How else could they survive?

These bodies from other realms aren't like ours, with filaments on their heads and algal scraps wrapped around them, holding their bodies together because they were made so weak. Why would you live someplace where you'd have to wrap your body just to stay safe or warm?

Without water, their land must be inhospitable. Wouldn't they suffocate in the open air? Or can they hold their breath for hours? If they venture from the coast, do they need to find pools of water where they can submerge their heads?

In the water, we know that sleekness isn't affected by your size. Can you imagine the spectacular sight of one of their whales charging across the terrain, undulating through the air with each silent, rumbling step? Would there be shoals of them across their plains? Whales are full of themselves, but that is one thing I'd like to see.

Otherwise, it could only be a sorry, infected place. So far from the ocean's depths, their world must be hot. We've felt the land's heat infect the sea. Do these creatures live in cities there, and do their cities disintegrate like the corals?

We know how hot it is around the volcanic fissures in the abyssal plains. Can you imagine what they're like without ocean water to cool them?

We know the more challenging life is where you live, the more intelligence you need to flourish there. The water is always changing. It has a billion variations, but the land stays where it is—unless it crumbles into the ocean (it must not be able to stand another moment there). So how intelligent can these creatures be if they keep living on land? When they pound the ground with their forelimbs, as Brola showed us, do they want to pound themselves? Don't they realize they'll break, with all those delicate and crunchable joints?

This one has already started to dissolve. Even in the water, it is filthy.

Without the free movement of the sea—without the grace of having it take you and sweep you away—these creatures must feel constrained. By their world, by the stillness, and by their own bodies.

If it needs to break, maybe that starts with needing to break free.

But maybe it also made pictures in the sand. If it could find some shells.

And maybe it also wanted to fly.

16

The ocean isn't empty space. It's entirety, and we're a part of that. The water is the origin, our present, and the future, and yet we know some of it keeps drifting up, atomizing into the infinite sky, before returning someplace else. It knows where it came from, like the salmon. It comes back.

Is there such a thing as emptiness above us, where the ocean's skin turns white before leaving on its journey? If the sky transports the molecules of our ocean, then it can't be empty. But it's for the birds.

The pounding continued. If the land creatures don't live in the ocean or the sky, what's left for them? Maybe land is nothingness, just sprawling plains. I hope there really are herds roaming across them, full of the quiet, incessant patter of their whales.

Waves don't stop as they pound at the shore and splash against the sky. So why would this other pounding stop now?

What really stops in the ocean? Except for an individual life.

I'd like to think I got better at drawing in the sand. As I said, I came up with my own technique. I'd shift my weight onto my tail, letting it settle against the ground and relying on it as a pivot. Then I'd use my pelvic fins to lower my body, adjusting and stabilizing with my pectoral fins if I got too close or the current pushed me to either side. Like that, I could bring my snout toward the sand. I grasped a broken staghorn coral branch between my teeth and used its hard edge to rake the grains. I'd have to shuffle backward as I drew, which wasn't ideal, but if I moved in the opposite direction, it would wipe away most of what I'd made. I can see now how having four limbs would be useful for propping yourself up on three and then still having the fourth one for drawing, or anything else. Of course, having six or eight limbs would be even better, but any more might get in the way.

Others had the same idea. By now, the creature's limb had come detached, which made it so much easier to use. Packs of adolescents watched Gjila scoop and scrape the sand with the clingers on the limb, and then they devised their own techniques. These days everybody wants to be different—as long as they can express their nonconformity while part of a group. They'd gather in uncluttered stretches and make fleeting shapes in the sand, before hurrying away to make more of them someplace else. Some switched back and forth between coral fragments while they worked on their designs, keeping branches of different circumferences and differently angled tips bundled together in blades of kelp, as kinds of drawing kits.

Yes, I admit, their designs were better. The young are always more adept at the new technology.

Occasionally, they'd work together, teaming up on projects, with two or three of them finning slowly along an image's outer edges, while they bounced one more of their friends between them, allowing that friend to focus on his drawing without worrying about finning himself into place or his tail getting in the way.

Sometimes, once the projects were done, they'd even push stones and shells around their designs to keep the currents from erasing them quite so fast.

I've seen some of them last for minutes.

The other thing you couldn't deny is that you could grasp a coral fragment in one of the creature's limbs better than you could in your mouth. Those little clingers at the ends didn't look very strong, but they were dexterous! The four main ones you could curl or push together or pull apart. You could even entwine them around each other like strands of sea rods or pull them backward until they looked ready to snap.

But the fifth one was different. It was as mobile as any antenna—and yet so much thicker. The base was more like the belly of a good-sized shrimp. Likely, it was as delectable. Sometimes we'll observe snow crabs grabbing small shells with their pincers—lobsters are able to do this, too—but they're limited to just a single movement and are happy if they're able to grip something, more or less (I've never known a crab who was a perfectionist, or a lobster who ever admitted anything was wrong). But you could imagine how these creature's clingers could work together to move a coral fragment exactly how you liked—spinning, twisting, or flipping it, while always staying in control. Or how the fifth clinger, with its smooth skin and more muscular base, would have been ideal for introducing into an anus.

So much better than relying on a cleaner wrasse to attend to your nether parts—especially one who could turn out to be a bluestriped fangblenny, if you weren't careful.

Because then you'd really need eyes on the back of your head. Like a flounder.

17

The ocean enters our bodies, through our eyes, our mouths, our nares, our skin, and our gills. To have slits along your neck is an open invitation, but I like to think we are more private, more guarded. More in control. We are our own deciders, and yet there is no way to close yourself to the world. The ocean circulates within us. It is our blood and muscles and organs and bones. It is our reanimation. When its minerals and oxygen and protozoa have been exhausted, the ocean flows out from us again. New ocean rushes in. There is restitution, an exchange, although we have other names for it, depending on which hole we use.

So how does this creature from land exist? It doesn't have gills for air. Or a blowhole. Maybe there's some special place it goes where the air is cleaner. It plans ahead. Until then, it holds its breath.

Galla* and Govili† nudged stones and shells with their snouts to the edges of their composition. The two adolescents tried to push them with their tails, but that didn't work. The smaller ones kept slipping past their fins. The process was fatiguing, but essential if there

---

*Gallā'holla.
†Govī'lī'niru.

was going to be any permanence to their work. They also used their teeth to move the shells. That method was more precise, but it took even longer.

Once there was a base, they added a second layer. The more stones and shells they used, the more protection the barrier would give to whatever they made inside. So they added another layer after that. The more fragments you used to build it, the farther you had to be willing to travel to get them. Better that you collected them before you started to sketch, because your drawing wouldn't last until your return.

Govili swam two body lengths back to get a better look. On one side, the barrier resembled a colony of star corals. But it also looked like a conger eel—it just needed a few adjustments around the jaw and fins. So Govili started fiddling. It's true he dismantled part of it, allowing the current to wash in. But no matter. Did it make any difference what had been inside? He kept making changes, embellishments. The currents didn't affect the frame, as they had his unprotected sketch, so he kept at it for days, adding pebbles, crunching on shells until the sizes were right, and then spitting them out and moving them to different spots.

Sometimes he was in a better mood than in others. He didn't eat. He lost weight.

18

We're not good at counting. There are seven tribes. That number is easy, even if we're not sure the Fantaskla exist. After that . . . we estimate. It's hard to keep the larger numbers in your head, since they aren't something you can smell. Maybe you feel them flit, or you catch a collective whiff. But that's only if they're living organisms, and when you talk about the entire ocean it only adds up to one. No one would expect you to count grains of sand, alterations in the current, or undulations of the sea floor. No one would want to. Occasionally, the Caavaju will offer precise numbers for something, like how many bridled triggerfish watched them snack on a sward of spiky sea urchins, but soon you realize they've just made it up. When a shoal appears, there's no way to count the fish— so it's not like there's an actual number. It's either a shoal or it isn't. Although it can be a very *large* shoal. Which is true whether they're mackerel or anchovies, even if the distinction isn't immediately obvious.

When discussing sharks, you can talk about a mouthful of teeth. So you need to identify the species, because each of them has a different number of rows, drastically changing how many teeth there are altogether. You see what I mean.

The number of protozoa can change a hundred- or thousand-fold just while you count. You'd have to count in circles, and then you wouldn't know where you started. Plus they move. And how do you count them without eating a few?

There are some exceptions:

Our hearts beat forty times per minute, so that's a number we know. That's how long it takes our blood to circulate through our bodies. We teach our young that that's how long it makes sense to fight the current: forty beats, or forty oscillations of their tails. Currents don't stop. They sweep through you, but you mustn't confuse them with emotions. They circumnavigate the globe, predictably and inevitably. You might advance against them, but eventually you'll tire and have to stop, and then you'll end up where you started, worse for the wear, and ready to be picked off by a shark. It's a losing battle. So when you feel the blood in your mouth return from your tail, recognize you've reached your limit. Accept it. Welcome it. That isn't giving up. You can't resist the water, because that's resisting the world. Giving up is stopping to eat or breathe.

Another one is the number of minerals in the water, once you enter the deep. That number is seventy-three, and it doesn't change even if you add a few or take some away. Potassium is generally my favorite.

The creature's limbs were still another. All those clingers together had to equal thirty or forty, if you included the puny ones on the lower limbs, sheathed by some extra skin. But when the forelimb was detached and you considered it by itself, you saw there were only five clingers on each of its ends. I don't know how many there would be if you had more (let's say it turns out the creature has a sibling, and they fused together during sex, like anglerfish do) or if the body could be put back together in other ways, but there are five of them now.

Five. Not as good as seven. Let others do the math.

19

Govili's creation was remarkable. By the time he'd finished, it was as if coral had spread in a full circle, as decisively as a tentacle. The form was made from at least several hundred stones and shells, thicker than an amberjack and as broad as a marlin. Did it matter anymore what had been inside? I'm not even sure Govili remembered—it was gone by the time his structure was complete. He tossed a few stray mollusk shells inside as an afterthought. Someone else had eaten them.

He looked thin. Arguably, that's what this kind of work will do to you. It makes you weak.

If work doesn't lead to catching food, making a nest, evading predators, or finding a mate, you might ask: What's the point? Why expend the energy? Even in our world of abundance, energy has its limits. But you couldn't deny that some of our younger females were charmed by Govili's efforts. They milled around, giggling. Occasionally, they'd come up to him and flirt. Now he would need his strength! Respond to a female right, and you can usually count on her to bring you food. Which is exactly what happened. One darted off and returned with a grouper. Another showed up with a pompano. A third arrived with a mouthful of kelp, but then slouched away embarrassedly.

Govili ignored them all. He kept adding to his structure, repairing it when individual shells tumbled from the outer layers, improving it where a given side didn't seem exactly right. He was more interested in the females who brought him stones and shells.

You might say he was a "user."

That attracted some females even more.

We want what we want. Some things don't ever change. Even now. They can't.

Then Brola approached, sweeping his tail across Govili's construction. Forty parabolic flicks take just one minute—exactly as many as you'd use against the current. There wasn't much left of the frame once Brola had finished. No, that's not right. All the pieces were there, so everything remained—and yet there was nothing.

Sharks began to circle. You didn't have to count their teeth.

20

The sharks tore into the grouper. Then they came for Govili. It wasn't clear if Brola had brought them, but it didn't matter once they were there. Let's just say Govili captured their attention, and, from that point on, sharks aren't easily distracted. Especially not once they're focused on your taste.

They charged. Four together, with more behind them. When a body is torn in two separate directions, it's over quickly. Add additional directions, and it doesn't necessarily go any faster, but there is more blood. Plus there's a sort of corporeal disintegration that is hastened by the currents. The body simply comes apart, although for a time each piece of it is still alive.

Sharks don't have names. At least, they don't answer to them. They answer to opportunity and weakness. And to blood.

They have teeth.

They snapped at Govili and gnashed and tore. He was gristle and skin and bone and blood, and even still a little bit of fat. Once he was also organs—lungs, liver, stomach, intestines, heart. Some animals will try to gulp the heart quickly to make sure a rival doesn't get it, but the sharks prefer crunching down to see it explode. Govili was and then he wasn't, just like the structure he had built—although those pieces remained, while suddenly he was gone. The sharks took off, as they do. The female suitors fled, with their pompano and kelp. Brola stayed.

What doesn't float away is gobbled up. Once the sharks are gone, there are many other creatures who will do it.

You used to say, "Gobble *me*." Those words had a different meaning then. They were play, they were tease. You were alive. I wouldn't say those words to anyone now. I can't say them to you.

You were full of life. Nervous and weak before giving birth, but with the impending glow of motherhood across your skin. Turn translucent, and we could even see our brood growing inside you, their wriggling bodies exploring the fluid—the first world they'd know, before emerging into the larger one. It's a dangerous place, sure. So many would die after they were born, but that's not supposed to include their mother, too.

Then you bled. The sharks sensed it.

Where was I? We talk so much about how there's just one ocean, but that includes its terrors, faults, and risks. I was hunting, trying to bring enough food back so I wouldn't need to leave again, just as my own parents had when I was young. Would my prey have asked about our love and our newborn kin? I was creating a memory I'd have forever. The salt water doesn't need our tears, but we add them anyway.

I'd left Gola to keep you company and protect you. He blocked the first shark as it came. They were bulls. It tore at his abdomen, and then he started floating up. He watched as you grew smaller and smaller, and then one of them tore at your abdomen, too. That's how he told me, when I pressed. He didn't want to say anything at first. Our brood spilling out into the currents, to be swallowed up in frenzied gulps. Then the bulls came back at you, until you were a cavity, the rest of you floating away.

I already knew what had happened as I approached, tasting your blood in the currents, the ferritin, leukocytes, glucose, and urea growing stronger as I neared. I raced, beating my tail and caudal fin as hard as I could, keeping my head and body streamlined, pressing my fins against my sides and using them only to stay on course. I smelled the many parts of you, stretched out over rocks and open water. I felt the first forty beats as my blood circulated through my body. Another forty, as it rushed through me again. Then another forty, faster. And another forty, faster. Faster. Until my muscles burned, my own heart trembled, and I passed out.

I didn't know where I was when I woke up, only what I had lost.

Now Govili's gone too, and I never even liked him. I'll have to think of him when I think of you.

I think of you all the time, and of *them*.

I don't want to talk about your heart.

21

Brola approached the disarray of stones and shells. During the attack, he'd snuck away and torn the other upper limb from the body. Now it dangled from his mouth like a piece of sponge, flapping in the current.

And yet everything had begun moving slowly. Brola swam slowly. I watched slowly. There is a kind of watching where you keep your head and neck fixed, while letting your eyes rotate in their sockets. (Unlike us, fish don't have necks. Their skulls attach directly to their shoulders. So it's not only intelligence that stops them from becoming self-aware. I keep reminding myself that this also is true for the sharks.) Although you see everything happening around you, there's only so fast an eye can turn. So you take things in deliberately and consciously, studying them as they occur, because you don't allow yourself the chance to look away. Brola raked the stones and shells with the five curled ends of the limb, scattering them effortlessly. It didn't matter how unhurriedly he moved. The limb disassembled the remains of Govili's structure in a matter of moments, and then the current did the rest.

You couldn't deny it: the creature's limb was unparalleled at taking things apart, at scattering them, and returning them to a state of nothingness. Brola held the limb in his mouth, as protective as a mother seal with her pup. Gjila appeared with the other one, just to emphasize that he had it.

They glared at each other, each of them armed.

Détente.

Then just as abruptly, it was over. Each retreated. That unraveling happened quickly. We know that time can progress at any speed. When a process appears gradual, it's usually because there are many parts, with each of them ending rapidly, in almost unending succession. Parts of parts of parts of parts. How many years does it take corals to grow? How many seconds to smash them to bits? Parts of parts, and parts of parts.

We know time moves faster closer to the surface, where there is the pull of the moon, corals die, algae spreads, and flesh decays. But on the ocean floor, where life processes slow down, you still find the throwbacks, the ancient creatures who couldn't live anywhere else. In the deepest part of the twilight zone, where I found the body, that depth should have been a comfort. The creature must have lost consciousness before it arrived, but some of its cells would still have been alive, and each of those cells is a world that also wants to survive. It was the same when I lost you there, too. The parts of your body I sensed and smelled, the ones still pulsing. In the before. But the remains of Govili's structure were the only things that had scattered across the sea floor fast.

The Banjxa talk a lot about speed. But I think the main advantage of moving quickly is to hide the things you don't want others to see. Maybe that is magic. The Banjxa don't like to linger in the deep.

Then Brola was gone. The structure, too. Had anything ever been there? Other than the existence of our young—and the scars we carry on our skin—is there proof that anything happens anywhere at all? The Akla scars are not just a rite of passage but of their existence, too.

I don't know what happened to the trevally I caught that day while I was hunting, before I realized the rest of my world had come apart.

The land creature seems so unimpressive, but it also has a neck.

22

We are each other's pets. We all want the same thing: to be protected, to be loved without conditions, to be entertained, to have companionship, to have someone soft to rub against, particularly when we're sad.

What is a lover? What's the difference between the two? When I was growing up, was I Gola's pet? He took care of me. I know that role gave him comfort and meaning. I loved him without conditions, as did my siblings. I know we were entertaining to him. But there's no way any of us could protect him. He didn't rub against us, as you hear about sometimes.

Was he our pet, too? He protected us—at least I know he tried. He provided warmth and companionship. Sometimes we swam to his side and nestled against him when we were lonely or scared. (When you're a single fry, the ocean can be a terrifying place, whatever your species.) But I don't think he'd like to have been called a pet. You're not a pet when you're the one in charge.

We did what he told us. If we didn't, that was a mistake none of us made more than once.

Then some of us died. The rest of us got older. Gola grew older, too. Parents turn into children, but pets don't become masters or vice versa. It's not the same thing.

True, pets swim off. That's a different story. I hope he comes back. There's only one ocean, so there's really no place else to go.

Were you my pet? Was I yours? If I'd suggested that, I suspect you would have bitten me. Of course, biting doesn't necessarily disqualify you from being a pet. Or something more.

Licking doesn't disqualify you from being that either.

We're in the ocean, so there's no inappropriate place to pee.

A relationship can be anything—it's just an association between two different creatures, and one of them can even be a parasite, like a tongue-eating louse inside a snapper's mouth. But a relationship has to mean you want to build—and that you're building it mindfully, with effort and intent. The obvious example of that is a family, but maybe it can also be a way of life. The way you understand your role in an ocean surging with myriad creatures, or how you swim headlong into the abyss, because you know that if left unattended curiosity can be a kind of parasite, too. (Maybe you can be in a relationship with yourself, but you can't ever be your own pet. So that's another difference.)

I'm not sure you have to be equals with your partner. I'm not sure you even have to be friends. You just have to keep on building and building. Taking what you have and turning it into something more. Or trying to, anyhow.

It's not success that matters, but the intent. Your ambition.

23

Where do we find meaning in our days, with no way to mark them? Are we supposed to catch it in the currents with our teeth and deposit it into our nests like bits of food? We act as if it's all around us, imbuing each flick of a fin and everything we do. That's undiluted shit.

We create attachments to one another. Then those attachments matter. We have offspring. That's a good way to create a thousand attachments all at once, even if we know most of them will die. The more we lose, the more we feel. Suffering makes us feel important, even special. That's shit, too.

You can trace your lineage back a thousand years, although no one can actually count that high. Then you can say your scions will inhabit the ocean for thousands more, but that only means you're raw material.

Many creatures in the ocean aren't self-aware. They're kelp, with moving parts. But does that mean they don't matter? No one likes to think that about themselves while they're being crushed against a rock or getting eaten while they're still alive. Or maybe you're lucky if you have those thoughts, because without them you're just shards and crumbs and ooze.

It's a great conceit to think the things you do are heroic. It's the greatest conceit to believe the things you do to make your own life better does the same for others. Does a predator improve life for his prey?

Is there meaning in generations spiraling out from your loins? Is there meaning in cellular accretions? Is there meaning in taking things apart?

Is any of this plausibly romantic? Or are we only supposed to talk of love and of the things we wanted?

24

Think what you want about Govili. The ocean is life and death. Isn't that the entire world? Is it any different where the creature comes from? Only the corals were supposed to live forever.

You can sink into the abyss, where everything stops moving in the cold, but is that the same as eternal life? If you ask the Banjxa, you can never feel as alive as when you're feeding, but that also means you're taking another's life. Once you reach the ocean's depths, there is no more plant life, no more kelp. Then the only food that exists are other animals. Like us, some of them have favorite colors and minerals. Often there are also some newborns and juveniles swimming around, getting into trouble.

All of us speculate about the creature's world and the weirdness of living out of the water. It hardly seems these beasts are made for much. They have the gooey, twisted bodies of sea cucumbers, with skin you can easily tear. Where are the muscles? How much strength can you build eating plants?

Scuttling around on those misshapen limbs beneath the noxious sky must be a piteous sight. It is hard to imagine there are many of them. We know our planet is mostly water, so where could they even go? If they became dehydrated, would there be anything of them left? And how could they stand living so close together? What we all need, more than anything else, is the healthy interplay of wriggling together and then staying far apart.

Some of us have a theory. These creatures must use their feeble limbs to erect structures to protect themselves from the dangerous and terrible things in their world: lava flows, air, earthquakes, predators, volcanic fissures. (You could easily tear the heads off these creatures, just as we did to this one's genitals and limbs, so perhaps they scavenge for abandoned shells to crawl into, like hermit crabs.) But maybe they build wonderful things, too. We adorn our females with seaweed and convince the silversides to swim around them as jewels, so could you create something that wouldn't float or swim away? And could you devise a way of conveying meaning without using your mouth? That would be especially useful if you lost your tongue.

Where do you put creativity, if not inside your mouth?

Govili's structure could have been bigger. All he needed were more stones, more shells, more helpers, more time. Here's what happened next:

The females who had watched him work, and then be torn apart, began returning to the site, one by one. What did they want? To find a souvenir? A memory? A scent? Colli* of the Caavaju found a shell—it had belonged to a clam—and she placed it where one side of his structure had stood. There was nothing to see in the sand, but you could smell its absence. Then Colli swam a few lengths away and returned with a whelk. Agara† of the Akla saw this, and

---

*Colli'hã'ique.
† 'Agã'ra'rēre.

she started placing stones and shells in the area, too. They didn't speak. Our dialects can be off-putting the first times you hear them. The two of them labored. The structure grew.

Then Bhoja[*] of the Banjxa approached from another group coalescing on the side, and she added a stone as well. But Colli didn't like where she placed it, so she moved it to a different spot. Bhoja disagreed. She picked it up and put it back. This time Agara swam over, and was the one to move it away. So Bhoja nipped at her. Nothing more than a bite of her pectoral fin, but nothing less. There was a hint of blood. Yes, creativity resides in the mouth, along the edges of our teeth.

It was two against one, with the possibility of the situation devolving further if anyone else got involved. More Gjala, Akla, Banjxa, and Caavaju arrived. They watched the growing fracas from all sides. I think a lot of them were ready to join in, and yet Colli, Agara, and Bhoja didn't seem to be fighting about anything important. It wasn't an issue of food or territory or nests or mates. There wasn't a threat to their young, and the threat to themselves was one they'd created. And yet the decision around the placement of each stone had become unforgivingly urgent.

Agara sank her teeth into Bhoja and then whipped her head back and forth.

One of the Banjxa raced to Bhoja's aid, looked around, seemed confused, and then swam away.

Bhoja wouldn't give up. As soon as she broke free, she hardly bothered to bite Agara back. Instead, she darted to the stone and returned it to the structure's edge, even while her peduncle bled, oozing into the water around her. I suppose you had to respect her

---

[*]Bhoj'ahōlla.

dedication—believing so fundamentally in your work that nothing would distract you. Now we had to wonder if the sharks would return for her, too. And was this *work*? Like herding plankton or lobsters for the promise of a meal?

Then another of the Caavaju left her pack and dug a shell out of the sand. She swam a few lengths away and put it in a different spot. Then she picked up another. Bhoja saw this—was there suddenly a nonconfrontational way to resolve the developing feud?—and swam to her side, arriving with her own stone. Imagine treating stones like they were precious objects and things you didn't want to lose! Both kept adding to the new site, and before long there was a second structure. Each of those formations continued to grow, as the stones and shells along their sides started piling up. Perhaps the brain corals sensed what was occurring. It would take them a thousand years to grow a minuscule fraction of what was being built around them now in two separate locations. But maybe more than envy, they felt impotence, too—the shaming inconsequence of inhabiting a boundless world where everyone in it surpasses you. But I don't think Agara was appeased. Or Colli.

Is this how battles start? Both groups wanted the same thing: to honor Govili and his memory. To do the same thing that he had. But to be the only ones to do it. And to do it better. Especially *that*. We tell our young that battles start when you don't want to share, and we put it to them that simplistically so that we're sure they'll understand. Only later do we also warn them about the dangers of seeking glory.

Both groups kept building. Days went by. Both built higher than Govili's original structure. You wouldn't say now that either group made frames. Both structures were closer in form to barrel corals, but misshapen and ugly. They rose as high as a lobster—and then three lobsters—rearing up.

Meanwhile, neither group ate.

Then finally there were no more shells or stones, at least none within a reasonable distance. So Bhoja swam away and returned with a chunk of red tree coral. It looked as if she'd ripped it from its base, feather stars adorning its branches. They'd die, all of them. And for what? Bhoja quickly placed the cluster atop her structure, and then she went to get more. Some of the Akla set off after her. They killed her quickly, four of them at her neck.

25

Gjila tells us, Do not fight for honor. Do not fight for vengeance. Do not fight about what's unimportant. But what about killing to keep others safe? What about fighting to protect the little guys, even if they're a mouthful of zooxanthellae and a displaced chunk of coral? We kill ciliates every time we eat. We kill them by accident every time we open our mouths, because to do so is to swallow water and that is life. But what if the truth is you just like to kill? You like to hunt? You like the thrill of watching a body go limp along the edges of your teeth, especially if there's also a little blood? Gjila does not condemn fighting for sport, and every time you fight you know you might kill or be killed. Real fighting is not play. It is creativity involving the muscles of your jaw and the sharpest serrations inside your mouth. Before you make another creature die, you make it dance. That is also art.

And yet I say we are peaceful. And this is a peaceful world. So what about killing to protect it? That's not something we've had to think about before. You can't kill volcanic fissures, earthquakes, or tidal waves. When the world is angry, you accept it. You let it take you where it will. If you survive, you just swim back. You see something new along the way.

If you're not going to accept life in our world, what's your other choice? Doesn't that acceptance bring a kind of inner peace?

We watch the whales and dolphins breach our world. What if you could swim so fast you could shoot from the water, through the air, and into the great universe of the aqueous unknown that must flow and surge beyond it? That would be a trick. Then you could just keep on going. But I don't think even the Banjxa can swim fast enough for that.

Bhoja had no choice but to die. Maybe it was because she was too eager to create a new world here, exactly as she wanted. Maybe it was because she killed the coral, and everyone knows they can't defend themselves. To be born as defenseless as coral is disgraceful. Even zooplankton can try to swim away. When did we need to start taking care of the world? It's always done that on its own, while also taking care of us. Don't the corals need some fucking teeth?

Agara and Colli went back to working on their structure. They dismantled Bhoja's, which meant there were more stones and shells for them to use.

They'd made a perfect frame by the time they were finished. Bhoja's head and twisted body fit easily inside.

26

Why didn't Agara and Colli also have to die? Because someone would have had to kill them. There are many possible answers, but that one's it.

The world is many things—up- and downwellings, gyres, ebbs, and flows—but it isn't fair. You can't have balance where there are also currents. In the ocean, many things float away. Only some return. No one chooses which ones he gets.

Sometimes the water sinks. It happens in the ocean's coldest regions. When two patches of water mix, and one is warmer and saltier than the other, the resulting water becomes denser and lower in volume than it was before, and so it starts tumbling down. It infiltrates. Your skin and teeth feel it. You can hear and taste it. The Banjxa would even say it has an infinitesimal effect on their speed.

That sinking launches the deepest ocean currents. It starts at the poles, where the frozen floating savory water is full of cod and krill. Then when that salty cold descends, slipping downward like a tongue, the warmer water takes its place, like a prospective lover sensing opportunity. Then the denser cold slides inexorably toward the abyssal plains, channeled by the crags and peaks, oozing toward the equator, before it can start heading up again. That interchange is how the currents start and how they continue. Interchange is relentless.

It's easy to get fixed in your ways, even in the ocean, even if nothing here is ever truly fixed. Not even if you are a barnacle, because you might be a barnacle on a whale and find your entire life is spent on a voyage. Is that how Bhoja got caught? Did the colder or newer water slow her down, or distract her from the currents? It couldn't as much as the stones and shells she clutched in her teeth. It couldn't as much as the disturbance of the creature who sank to us, with different salinity and body temperature, interrupting everything we knew. Or we thought we did.

The facts don't matter as much as their interpretation, because there's no one who can say who's right. The only thing we can know for sure is that the ocean is omnipresent. When there's rain on the surface, it's proof there's more ocean just beyond it. Or that our ocean is the only one, its pull is irresistible, and the water keeps coming back.

27

Water moves where it chooses. Life moves where water brings it. You can't attribute everything to downwellings and the tides. Birth is chance. So is survival. But each of us knows that death is coming, and we congratulate ourselves by saying that's the advantage we have over the fish.

We live in a world of doltish creatures, with no sense of consciousness beyond their desire to eat, not to be eaten, and to spawn. They don't understand our problems. There's no sophistication. They see, but they don't perceive. No one in the ocean mistakes the ability to navigate large distances for actual intelligence, since you can do that with your eyes closed.

The creature comes from a world compressed between two oceans: ours and the rest of it in the great beyond. It must live under a lot of pressure, relentless grinding from above and below. The only certainty is it must scuttle from side to side, like a crab.

Or maybe it has found a way to use its clingers to build a structure into the sky and pierce the film separating it from the celestial ocean. (We already know there are holes in it, because that's what lets in the storms—but perhaps the film regenerates, just as mucus does around a fish.) How many stones would you need for such a monstrosity? It would have to be a mammoth tower to reach the babbling water on the other side, like a geothermal spire of silica and diatoms rising from the ocean's floor. And naturally it would eventually fall. There'd be no water to press against its sides and hold it together.

Do you think there are the ruins of mysterious toppled towers across the creature's land, and that sometimes they crush the ones underneath? To die that way is less personal than to be eaten, and it is wasteful. At least being consumed by another creature gives meaning to your death.

Birth is chance. Death is certainty. But how death arrives—that is also chance.

We all watched Bhoja become a collective meal. I couldn't resist her tail, although many prefer the pectorals for their combination of muscle and fat. There's no point to eating sullenly. Flesh is celebration. Anything less is disrespectful of the animal that gave its life, regardless of whether that gift came willingly. Or with substantial pain. Meat is a feast. Beware the vegetarians by the surface. They are individualists, loners. Some of them are fanatics.

Did Bhoja understand she was going to die? Surely she felt the rise in tensions, and she'd have sensed the others approach—the tingle of their magnetic fields growing closer, accompanied by their creative and infinitely expressive teeth. Perhaps she ignored them at first, but you can't do that once they start biting down. Not even the sea cucumber is staid when it's being split in half. Plus Bhoja tasted more like bigeye tuna. (Like tuna, we're warm-blooded. That's what makes our muscles capable of speed and also delectable, not just to the sharks.)

Does the dying animal, grasping that its life is about to end, ever enjoy a nibble of itself? Can that ever be a final solace, enjoying the meat you've nurtured on your flanks your entire life? We're taught not to think about such things, but what is there to stop you? Your mind wanders before you die, so some thoughts are unavoidable.

Did I eat you? A bite. It made me sad.

And then another.

But I knew I had to. What else would become of your body?

Do the land creatures do that, too? Or do they allow opportunities to go to waste? Sadness is inevitable, even if how it blooms inside you is a matter of chance. Sadness comes at you like a current, but eventually it washes away.

Not all of it, though. You are my conscious, eternal proof.

28

Think of sadness and love, and of constructing mountains or towers one shell at a time. Then also think of breaking them.

Of sending them crashing down.

Then think of breaking that sadness and love as well—because both of those you also need to build. You shape them with whatever you have, your clumsy mouth and heart and fins, even if they stay as transparent as the water. But you know they're there. They remind you. They're insistent. And neither one of them you ever truly want to disappear. Because there is no love without a hint of sadness, and no sadness if first there hasn't been whirling, bracing love.

Was this creature missed? Did it miss someone before it died? If you're not missed, is there any proof you existed?

If you *are* missed, does that mean you only exist for as long as the memory remains? What if you're remembered but not missed by anyone at all?

Our creation myths—the Banjxa's ridiculous legends about a gargantuan octopus whose detached limbs gave birth to each of our tribes, or the stories we tell ourselves of the great-great-great-great-great-grandparents nobody we know ever met—does it mean those beings still reside among us, if their memories do as well? And if they were invented (perhaps that great-great-great-great-great-grandparent wasn't as benign or beautiful or brave as we've been told, and the giant octopus was more of a midsized cuttlefish), does that mean they exist now as they do in our stories, even if they didn't before?

I suppose it's the same thing with the structures, like the ones Govili, Bhoja, and the others built. There was a time when there was just the sandy ocean floor. Then each of them created something enduring. Those structures left their marks even after they were destroyed. Now they're memories, except that you can still see them. They smell and taste like absence, too.

After you died, I kept building your memory in my head, letting it stretch across me like an encrusting coral. I was afraid I would forget things, and you would fade. I talked and talked and talked to Gola, because I wanted him to remember everything there was about you. He promised he would—but *of course* he would. How couldn't he? He'd loved us both, he was ready to care for our children, and, before that, he'd cared for me. So he only said those consoling words to me out of abundant love. He made promises about things that were obvious and expected, but which I kept needing to hear.

I saw him eat you, too.

Where is he now?

We have this creature in Gola's place. We've built it up in our minds, created a story of where it came from and how it lived, and what it thought and knew and felt. And what it wanted.

We've talked about it so much that its body is a kind of current.

Was it intelligent enough to want to love? There are many creatures in the ocean who don't know what love is. There are others who know about it, but aren't sure they should want it. And others still who don't understand how to get it. But the last group are those who don't know how to keep it. Maybe those are the stupidest creatures of them all, because they are the closest to having what they want, and yet they still think they are intelligent, no matter how much they fail.

We mate for life. So all you have to do is stay alive.

29

I'm one of those creatures who didn't know how to keep it.

30

It has an unpronounceable name and scuttles across the ground, wheezing and grunting. It fornicates with plants and stones and other creatures, unable to recognize its own species as its natural mate. It's a biological anomaly, destined to disappear from the world like the panderichthys, a ridiculous fish if ever there was one. Imagine having an entire ocean, and then being stupid enough to crawl onto land.

It breathes air. Disgusting. It probably shits in the air, too.

If I had to micturate in the open air, at least I'd do it into my mouth. What if there were children watching?

The farther you are from water, the dirtier you are. That's an undeniable fact. *That is science.* You need the water to run over you, but also through you. Whatever's not firmly attached to you goes. Ablution and absolution. It's not our world, anyway. It's the water's. We just live inside it and invent horror stories about it disappearing one day for amusement. Maybe the water hasn't always existed. It's reasonable that everything starts somewhere. A place, a time. That's true for us. It's true for *it.*

I imagine on land everything just piles up. There's nothing to wash extruded or discarded things away. Does that help you build? Maybe it does. Perhaps this creature lives in agglomerations of its own filth, extracting whatever drops of water it can from its slime, and constructing homes from what is left. Then it sings love songs to its plants, the objects of its passion. No one I know would sing a love song to kelp—it's foolish to believe the plants would reciprocate.

But this creature comes from an earthen world, where its customs may be different. The heaps of this creature's houses must be its cities. They must crumble and sprawl. It must be accustomed to living in sloughs and floes of waste. That must be what it likes and what it longs for. It must dream only of debris.

Better that its gonads were removed, even if it was dead. You can't be too sure, especially with the weird anatomy.

31

Waves slurp at the coasts. Once, I slurped your skin. Before they break, the waves froth and coalesce, before tumbling and disappearing. I was the same.

After the attack, I wanted to dissolve into the rest of the ocean. You were gone, dispersed, and I was ready to sink. How do you fill something like loss when the world you live in is cavernous, too? We survive in emptiness. What if that vastness then suddenly becomes too big? Only the ocean floor could keep me from sinking farther. That's where I'd join the frigid abyssal ooze, and slip beneath it like a blanket, and count my heartbeats until they stopped.

Gola saved me.

He followed me as I descended. Then he warned: "Too deep."

It's true. The light was gone—the ocean water was only squid ink there. But what was there for me to see? After the first hundred sweeps of your tail toward the ocean's bottom, you don't even have to continue swimming. The gravity takes you. You give yourself to it.

You give in. You give up. I sank.

Gola chased me through the water column, and he bit into my back.

"Feel that, loser?"

He had to know I wouldn't have patience for his games.

He bit again.

"Leave me alone!"

"Tell me why I should do that, loser?"

"I lost them all."

"You think that makes you—what is it, *special*?"

"I can't . . ."

"I can't do *this*? I can't do *that*?" He grinned to show his teeth. "You lost them all. So what?"

"You ask me that? How dare you! I hurt. I'm sad."

He bit me harder. "Maybe you'll hurt a little more now. Sadly."

"I'm not going to fight you, Gola."

"That's good," he sneered. "Because I'm not particularly interested in your fighting back." Then he bit down again, with the annoying ferocity of a school of bigeye barracudas. I felt his swarming teeth.

"Stop it, Gola!"

"Why?"

Another bite. This time drawing blood.

"I said to stop it!"

"Why do you care? I'm hungry. Let me swim around in front of you, so I can get at your cheeks."

"*Aeeow,* Gola . . . that hurts!"

"You mean those bits I'm taking? I thought you couldn't feel any more loss—and it's not even like I'm going for your eyes. You know, if you'd ascend a little, to where the water's warmer, you'd heal that much faster, and then I could start eating those parts again."

"Stop it!"

"Don't be selfish, loser! I thought I raised you better!"

"Leave me be!"

"Yes, I know I raised you better. But if that's how you're going to be, then I'm going to start going for the bigger pieces. You can die just like she did, loser. Isn't that what you want?"

What did I want? For the pain to be finished. Surely that. But not just for the pain to disappear, but for the loss that caused it never to have happened. And to have now what you and I—*we*—always imagined. Wasn't that the ocean's plan for us, and ours? From that same moment when we met. Or even before. From when I sensed and smelled and tasted you. Which was impossible. I wanted the impossible. I wanted the inconceivable. All those fathoms down, I wanted what was unattainable now.

"I'm going to keep biting. Let me show you."

And I wanted to be whole.

"I just want the bit in front of me. Hold still. You'll hardly notice afterward you're missing that fin."

And the impractical. I dodged him.

"Now you're working up my appetite!" Gola jeered. "You think I'll be satisfied with a fin? Your loins look better. Now *those* look tasty."

I shoved him hard with my tail. He came back at me with his teeth, gnashing. I swam around him. He stalked.

I looked at him, nonplussed. "I can outswim you, Gola."

"You'd have to want to, though. That's why I'm going to eat you here."

He came after me and chased me toward the surface, where the colors embraced us—blues and greens and oranges and reds—against the warm, oily sweetness of the minerals and salts.

"It's better here, isn't it?"

I didn't answer.

"And here there are other things I can eat."

He swam away. I almost chased him.

32

You always swim faster with live animals in your mouth. They can be your offspring or your prey. You feel them ricocheting against your palate. Against your cheeks. Even your own fry want to escape. But you know better than to let any of them go. Their presence is a reminder of your role as a parent. Their movement gives you strength. Their flitting gives you speed. Perhaps they give you indigestion—when you have a mouthful of fry, you might end up swallowing a few by chance. Is that bad parenting? Sure. But it doesn't matter. There still are enough of them left, and they are safe.

When it's prey inside your mouth, it is another story. The living twisting pieces are the thrill, trickling with blood and excitement and hope. You devour their muscles. You gulp their organs. You crunch their bones, and swallow everything down.

They can be your prey or your kin, but once your mouth is empty, you want to fill it again. This must happen quickly.

33

Avoid the surface. Red tide sweeps in like rage. We know it's thickest at the surface where all fault lies, before it radiates down into our realm. It is wickedness, plague. To stay away has always been our advice. It's where the two-armed dinoflagellates commit their swelling and surging type of violence.

It is bad enough for the tide to seep through your skin and become a part of your body. And then to go through life knowing that's inside of you. No one talks about the pain, but the embarrassment.

The sun also finally needs to learn to keep its distance.

And then there's the wind, which bothers everyone but the gargantuan whales and the flying fish. What good are those gusts, except when they are cold enough to leave the ocean sealed—and the water beneath the frozen mantle clear? When our young are hurt, we teach them not to peck at the protective coverings that form across their wounds, or their friends'—even if they are delicious.

Barriers are the best defense, and sometimes they are the only ones. But all shells can be penetrated. The crab is not invincible.

Brola came barreling in with his thugs, slashing like swordfish, lunging and thrashing, creating confusion and tumult wherever they could, breaking up schools, finning up gravel, and smashing nests, along with some collateral impaling. The first taste of blood belonged to the mackerel. They'd brought them with them—their hearts still pulsing in their bodies, wedged inside the Banjxa mouths. It was meant to rile us, but one sniff gave them away. It was so stupid that it was funny. Until there was blood of our own, and then it wasn't funny.

I'd already lived through this once.

This time there weren't any sharks.

There were only Banjxa and Ecdda, our own attacking, our own being attacked. And our own witnessing it too, and remembering. How can you hope to forget, when the memories are in the water? I heard Gola's voice in the back of my head, but I didn't need him to urge me on. We fought back, all of us, but we were surprised and unprepared. Some of the Banjxa carried bills or bones in their mouths, and they used those on the nests without looking first inside.

A baby screaming in the water is loud and sharp and then silent.

34

Loser. All of us now.

35

A parent's voice repeats itself. It disappears and then returns as a peal, arguing the same things over and over. The variations are all the same. It is the clicking and crackling of snapping shrimp. Nothing is new, because nothing can be new, because anything new washes the old away. Besides, answers still haven't arrived, and so there are only questions. And sometimes there aren't words, which makes answering impossible. There is just ebb and flow of sadness and anger. Both of those you can smell.

Digging is loss unless you fill it. Breaking is loss until you rebuild.

I have many brothers and sisters. We have drifted away. I have many cousins. I don't know their names.

We Gjala have fewer children than we did before. It is an uncountable number. Mating won't change that. It can't. The loss is unbearable, and yet we will survive it with wrath and guilt. We will sniff the water for our young's remains and feed on their flesh with each agonizing bite until the last particle of them is gone and we carry them inside us, as bone, muscle, and resolution.

In the land creature's world, do they ever think of starting over? Do we?

Part 3

36

Then came the dirges. The wails and drones and yowls. The beating of the fins and the breasts. Songs of agony and sorrow. And finally the talk of reprisal.

The Banjxa would be ready and expect an attack. Our fastest swimmers would enter their waters. Their troops would meet them, carrying the same swordfish bills and bones in their teeth. Again, there would be a show of horrors, of what they could pound and beat and break—except they wouldn't disturb their own nests. But as fast as the Banjxa can swim, they'd be slowed by what they carried. And this time, they wouldn't have the element of surprise. So our swimmers would taunt them, snap and tear at their fins, and send them careening into crags and trenches with relentless sweeps of our tails, until the Banjxa would have no choice but to release the bones to recover their sleekness in the water. And then more of our Gjala would swoop in from all sides and pick them up. And we'd do the same to the Banjxa nests as they did to ours, with those bones and bills, and we'd see how they liked that.

Did I say once we were creatures of love?

Another plan: We'd hurtle in with all our numbers, in a show of blinding force. And rage. And the Banjxa would naturally cower in their nests from our astonishing, paralyzing display. Or we'd barrel in, they'd choose foolishness and bravado and swim out to meet us, and a battle would ensue. Paeans would be written about the confrontation. About the vengeance and the blood, the hearts sucked out of the Banjxa bodies and displayed before their failing eyes. Brola especially would be our quarry. We would hunt him, excise his heart from his chest, and explode it between our teeth, with the kind of crushing bites the sharks understand. We'd chew the muscle and spit the mashed pieces from our mouths, so they sank to the floor and drifted in the current. Maybe the goatfish would want them. The remaining Banjxa could eat the goatfish, if they chased them before they all swam away.

The sharks would come. The erupting hearts would be irresistible. They'd hear the percussive calls, even once those muscles had been turned to pulp. Then they'd turn on the Ecdda, who would have also entered the Banjxa waters, after they'd finally grasped the mightiness of our force—and the wisdom of turning on the Banjxa, too. Not that the Ecdda are known for their wisdom, which is why they wouldn't have anticipated the duplicitousness of the sharks. But are you ever supposed to regard a shark with trust? Entire flanks and ribs and fins pulled away from bodies until the ocean was soup. Not a single Ecdda left alive. Free-floating tails in the currents.

There would be some sharks dead, too.

Or maybe it wouldn't work out like that exactly. We Gjala are not butchers. The battle would go differently. Many of us dead, in addition to the Banjxa and the Ecdda. Or *instead* of the Banjxa and the Ecdda and the sharks, which would be worse. Our fry who hadn't been killed would be parentless now. Gjila says not to fight for honor. But should you fight if you aren't sure you'll win? Is it weakness to worry about the survivors?

Then came the dirges.

37

Why did the Banjxa and Ecdda attack? No, that's not a fair question. There are millions of Banjxa and millions of Ecdda, and only a few from each tribe were involved. Maybe hundreds or thousands, to be precise.

It's easy to understand the Ecdda's involvement. They are brutes, which makes them predictable. They're incapable of passing up a fight. That's not entirely bad, if you consider the fighting by itself. You could enter into a brawl and always be sure to end up on the winning side, because you'd switch allegiance at a moment's notice. If not for honor, you'd fight for victory. Forgive the pun, if you think that sounds shallow. But that's not even who the Ecdda are. The Ecdda fight for participation.

The hermit crabs know their carapaces aren't enough. Their abdomens are particularly susceptible to attacks. That's why they seek out abandoned shells, ones that are harder than their own. But when they find another hermit crab whose adopted home looks particularly durable or comfy, they're willing to kill the owner and take it for themselves. Hermit crabs are social animals. They live in colonies of the hundreds. But that isn't for mutual protection.

They need dupes and victims. Maybe the most narcissistic crabs need others to watch.

We Gjala talk of love. It's the choice of an embrace, when all other possibilities between two creatures exist. When two mouths meet, anything can happen. New species can emerge. Tribes can grow and spread through the ocean. We know those additional mouths are going to meet in time. We talk and kiss and eat and bite. Sometimes we even plan ahead. Each of us decides what he says and does, what she says and does. The ocean is ebb and flow. You get what you give. We talk of love.

38

Ooo, the ur-octopus the Banjxa believe in, was supposed to have given birth to us all. When its tentacles separated from its body, they became each of our tribes, while the eighth one vanished. For the Banjxa, Ooo became our world.

What do we believe in? That our world is glorious and peaceful? I don't know.

To see an octopus's tentacles pulled from the rest of its body is a grisly sight. The way the skin and muscles stretch, the massive power each of the tentacles has, the suckers grasping vainly at teeth and water, the colors and contours changing into an uncountable progression of aggression, defense, and desperation. The eyes, especially those.

Then the moment the body comes apart. The reverberation of the oozy snaps. The tentacles curling into themselves protectively, like bristleworms, as if the body and they can still survive, while hemorrhaging into the currents. The eyes and beak are the only parts that don't change color. But they all change color.

We say we are creatures of love.

Would the land creature say the same? Would it say the same about us?

39

We did this. Our Gjala. We are the Ecdda, and the sharks. As the Banjxa say, all of us come from the same place—whether it's Ooo's arms or the same forgotten cave. We are the Banjxa, too.

We bring destruction. Sometimes we tell it nicer. But each time there is an abyssal storm, or one swooping down on us from above, we know our world will be broken into pieces. That is the way. The corals are first. But they're not the only ones to feel it. To feel the ocean's wrath is to be a part of the ocean's wrath. All of us are products of our upbringing. The ocean is tempestuous. That's also who we are.

The octopus was severed as a message. As a warning. As disrespect. I can imagine it took a Gjala on each arm. Plus more to watch.

Wasn't there anyone to stop it? To say, "Swim away."

I don't know when it happened. I don't know how you'd decide to be a part of that. No one will admit to it.

To be the one who took a tentacle in his teeth . . .

To be one of the eight.

How beautiful that we can sense each other's feelings, or we'd have to talk twice as much. You can taste emotion. You can hear a heart beating beneath the sand. But there are also truths and facts, and questions that are an embarrassment and answers that will float away. You only need to wait for a current.

We eat octopus. We don't look them in the eye.

We gather in the canyon, what we call our temple, our prayer house. The encrusted tomb. Where the water is deep enough that nothing happens fast, and everyone's dream is of burying themselves in the goo. Every one to two thousand years, our planet's oceans mix through circulation. (Yes, one to two thousand is a number we know.) In two thousand years, we'll all be the same, but for now the differences among us are unmanageable and shocking. And widening. Two thousand years is longer than I'm prepared to wait. We're used to changes happening in a flash.

When one fish darts in a new direction, the others follow—or they don't. The first to leave the group leads a school, or it becomes a loner. If a school defects, it becomes a shoal. There are schools within each shoal, of like-minded fish that swim in the same direction, but when there are too many schools, the shoal breaks apart.

That's what happened to us. Our school became a shoal. It became our tribe. But we all started in that cave. We didn't start out as seven.

Would some of our Gjala become a new tribe now? Of octopus killers? Would they call themselves that? Or would they become so fixated on savagery that they'd become Ecdda instead?

Imagine a way to force a creature to stay in one place. To make it stay for days or years. That would be impossible. In the ocean, there is only motion. Not even the corals manage to stay in one place, no matter how hard they try. Storms are inevitable, unpredictable, and certain.

We can be solitary or social. You can learn a new dialect. Maybe you'll always have an accent or a peculiar way you express yourself. Sometimes that may be considered charming. Other times the creatures you choose to live among will laugh at you. Cruelty generally starts in the mouth. Not just along the teeth, but at the tongue.

Every creature spends its moments of life trying to avoid death—whether to outwit it or escape it. Is that consciousness? Knowing there's death just around the corner, and then not thinking about it? Not even when you eat.

An octopus can regrow its arms, if you give it time, if it gets a chance. That is easy. So is love. We think it's so natural we can grow it. But peace is the most complicated thing there is.

The octopus's tentacles taste like shame, but their bodies are still a delicacy.

40

Long before the fighting and the creature, when we were all a single shoal, the Dilidi broke away. Or perhaps they glided. Where are they now? They don't have territories of their own. They never wanted any. If you can't stay still in the ocean, why even try? Water doesn't move randomly. Neither do they. They swim slowly and indulgently, paying attention to the flutter and twists of their fins and their tails.

The Dilidi are everywhere and nowhere, but when the creature was found, they kept their distance. They weren't fearful, suspicious, or even particularly curious. They just didn't think the creature looked like fun, with the way its limbs and gonads dangled listlessly about its body before we tore them off. (Yes, dolphins like to find unusual things to play with and drag them around in their mouths, but the Dilidi are more discerning.) They're more captivated by games of chance, and songs, and trips, and extravagant meals, and procreation. They like to dance, shimmying and twirling in the water column. When arguments occur among others, they stay neutral. Perhaps that's one reason they never desired a territory of their own. They play so much because nothing in their lives has a stake. And because they play so much, nothing in their lives has a stake. But you can't reason with them about that.

They ask, "If we were more serious, would we be more fun?" And the answer is no, because they are exactly as much fun as an endless game, an endless song, an endless trip, an endless meal, or endless sex. Everyone wants to be a Dilidi, but not exactly without an end. Many go to live among them, but not all stay. Those who return come back without any territory and become outliers. They try to replicate the easy life they left behind, but there are too many distractions, and having multiple mates, of which the Dilidi are fond, only leads to trouble. Still, we sought them out.

41

No one is in charge underwater. Or another way to put it is the water is in charge. It knows precisely where it's going. And nobody would be stupid enough to try to stop it. Yes, there are dominant and submissive lobsters and sexual hierarchies among a wide array of fishes. Male clownfish become female, female wrasses become male, but no one forces another fish to change gender, because doing so would be obscene and sadistic.

Most creatures will fight to defend their territory, but it's always seemed so small-minded since there's enough space here for everyone, and the ones who are the most aggrieved are usually concerned about the smallest tracts. Maybe you prefer one ledge to another, or a particular anemone you've been nestling in has always seemed an inviting host, but the ocean is vast and much of it looks the same. If one spot doesn't have everything you need, you can always go somewhere else.

But we fight to defend ourselves and our fry. That's different. It has to be. Because then we'll fight to the death.

There have never been any power structures within our tribe. We live in communities spread out from one another, but we don't have leaders because none has ever been necessary, and how would you choose? Fight? Give speeches? Swim the fastest? Hunt the best? Be the biggest, as if the luck of what's passed down to you from your parents should matter most? It all seems so stupid. And then what would you do if you were in charge? Tell others where to swim? Take their catch from them, when getting your own will usually require less work and end up being fresher? Sometimes someone will give advice, as Gjila does. And if others think it's worth listening to, they'll let you know they're open to hearing more. In our language, Gjila is called a *hali'kā*, or a mineral-giver. Gola was one for me, too.

When I found the creature, I wanted to speak out. I'd gone out that day to be with you, wanting the impossible, and I found a different strange and impossible instead—one that also hadn't been able to survive. When representatives from the other tribes arrived, I hoped they would hear me and that the creature's discovery could bring us together, even if we didn't understand yet how far we'd drifted apart. But there was more to it than that. There was suddenly something new among us, and I hoped that thinking hard enough about it would fill a hole and even somehow bring a part of you back. Maybe not immediately, but the way sediment seeps in pebble by pebble, until a concavity is gone. It's even faster with the water. The ocean rushes into the nooks outside your skin, but the ones inside you don't fill as easily. That water has no volume. It disappears. So I spoke up when our tribes gathered together. Did we need a leader now? I don't know. But we had to respond.

The opposite of *hali'kā* is *da'nāhai*, or empty water, which our science tells us isn't supposed to exist.

42

I'm not sure what we thought would happen. Gjila and I went to find the Dilidi. I urged him to accompany me, but I also thought he'd be helpful once we were back. I don't know if *hali'kā* is a word other tribes use.

Like us, the Dilidi don't follow any organizational structure, although what you say to one quickly spreads through the water. We'd count on that. They do what they like, and sometimes when they're in the middle of an activity, you have to fin and wait before you get their attention.

It's amusing to watch two creatures having sex. Listening to them sing nonstop is another story. Watching them gorge themselves relentlessly is only marginally better, but it bothers you for longer.

We swam for days, dodging vents and seamounts, and peeking into ridges; listening, smelling, and trying to sense the crackle of their electrical fields. Since the Dilidi have never sought any territory, finding them takes both patience and some luck. On our third day, Gjila and I came across a trio huddling along a ridge in the Philippine Sea, betting on how many spider crabs they could stack atop one another. Naturally, the crabs kept trying to scramble away, and it was only after several escapees were cracked in half and swallowed that the remaining ones understood the value of remaining still—although they would sometimes fall and then obediently try to scuttle back into place. Because the quantity of crabs had grown so large, and the column now lurched like a giant rib, the actual number had become uncountable, which riled the Dilidi because there was no way to win. This provided us with an opportunity to interject, although it was rare to meet Dilidi who were so ill-humored. They seemed surprised by this as well.

"Cousins," Gjila began, "we trust you are enjoying yourselves?"

"The greatest pleasures don't involve trust at all."

"Will you let us know what we can do to help?"

"As you can see, we are coping with the poor sportsmanship of the crabs. They're foolish if they think we'll play with them this way again." The Dilidi leaned toward a group clambering at the base of the stack and snatched one crab up with his teeth. "But I think they will miss it."

"When you start randomly picking them out to eat," the second one added, "they become so much more attentive to the subtleties of the game."

"And to their nuances, really."

"Brothers," Gjila tried again, "I'm sure you realize it isn't a game of chance that brings us here, although I recognize it is our great fortune. You're aware of the land creature?"

"We prefer the crabs," the third one scoffed. "Especially their legs. Even with all their shortcomings, they're so much more solicitous about our pleasure." He ate another in two quick crunches. "They're delightful, really. Once they understand the stakes."

"Of course, they've been enjoying themselves at our expense until now," the first one said. "They're tasty, yes. But they depend on us to keep them entertained and to give their lives a sense of meaning."

Is this when we were supposed to tell them about the Banjxa and the Ecdda, and the violence committed to our nests? Or that was spreading through them now? But I suspect the Dilidi would have been able to sense it. They'd have felt our agitation even before we reached their camp. Perhaps we also are not good at keeping secrets.

Then the first one continued: "Don't tell me you've come this way to complain about your misfortunes." He nodded toward the stack, which had already begun to teeter, while simultaneously slinking away. "Isn't life already hard enough for us all? When all we want is a little order? And don't you see, if we ate them all now, we'd be left without our game."

"Or are you here because you're hungry?" the second one asked. "It's always so unpleasant to be hungry, but you must understand the crabs have given themselves to us and not to you."

"Besides, so many of the meatier and juicier ones are already lost. I mean this in a moral sense. So we need to protect the little ones and give them a chance to grow."

"It's the ones you don't see who are always the most at risk. That's true even when they aren't crabs. Although it's more meaningful to us when they are."

"Look, I know you think your problems are serious," the first one added, "but I'm sure you've heard what everyone says about the Gjala." He sucked a pair from the column's crest. Then, with their pincers and legs thrashing outside his mouth, he tossed in, smugly, "And more times than you can count."

43

There were other Dilidi, but it would be the same. We tried, of course.

It didn't matter where we went, how many vents and pillars we checked behind, or how many ridges we followed. We thought we'd just have to tell them our story, but they already knew it. We thought they'd want to know more about the creature, but they didn't. The only thing you could say with certainty is we didn't understand as much as we thought.

I was wrong: watching five Dilidi having sex while you're trying to talk to them about the destruction of your nests and the murder of your children is much worse than watching them eat for hours. The experiences are not comparable.

You would think that at least one of them would listen to you while the remaining four were occupied, but that is not the case.

They felt us approach every time we neared, and they were only surprised when we interrupted and didn't just keep swimming by.

44

Starting a conversation doesn't mean you will finish it.

The octopus can change its shape to become almost anything, but in the end it will always go back to being itself. If you let it.

When you were alive, so was the entire ocean. The water was thick with your salt and smell and grace and tang, and with your softness and your song and my desire.

The ocean wrapped around us. The currents were predictable. I wanted to wrap around you, too.

The coral spawn was a memory, a sweet one, an opening act that led to admissions, questions, quarrels, and discoveries, about each other and ourselves. We were going to create new life—ours, our fry's—but love isn't just biological function. This deep in the ocean you expect it to have depth as well. It is desire mixed with melancholy, because it is gratefulness and chance, and the foreknowledge of eventual loss. And bliss and chance.

I don't know if love can exist outside of the ocean. Here it has weightlessness, empathy, gravity, electromagnetism, and tentacles. I don't know how it would react with air.

Our cousins say we love too much, that we're addicted to that feeling, just as the Ecdda are to rage, the Dilidi to their inexhaustible pleasures, the Caavaju to themselves, the Akla to their rites of passage, and the Banjxa to impulsiveness and speed. And all of us to the dream of the Fantaskla, since none of us know if they exist. We want them to.

The creature is another question. There were always stories about the changes to our world and about what scurried beyond it, in that place where everything was inhospitable and dry.

You didn't need the creature's limb to pound. You could do that with a marlin's bill or bone. You didn't need it to sketch in the sand. You could do either of those without it. But the truth is you could do both of them better—and more accurately—if you had the limb fixed between your teeth. Never mind the bones and tendons slipping out.

Of course, the creature only had two of those upper limbs. Most life is symmetrical, until an injury occurs. If Gola were around, he'd have something to add about that. We tried using the ones in back, but they weren't good for drawing. They were more like tails, but limited in how they flexed, which made them harder to control.

Not all creatures have faces, the focal points of those matched proportions, which always converge between the eyes, unless you're a flounder. This one was lucky. It's a sign of evolution to have a face, or even a front. But that leaves your posterior open to a sneak attack. The butterflyfish have those garish eyes on their flanks to fool the stupid. We have tails to wallop you with instead.

The creature must have been defenseless. It could barely bite with that fragile jaw, and those fleshy and symmetrical lips would have been irresistible to anyone passing by. What choice would it have had but to pound and flail with its limbs? And to spear and swipe and swing and poke?

It's easier to break things than to put them back together. We know that. Building something new is almost impossible, so we build the same things over and over. We build nests. We build families and lineages. If we don't build relationships, at least we build desire. We build those stupid frames.

Imagine if you could put someone you loved back together. Or anyone at all. Then their face could go on forever. At least as a picture in the sand. The world would be what it isn't now and wasn't before, and it would be perfect.

The Caavaju say our world can be perfect because there is only one, but they haven't answered how they can all be perfect themselves, if they number into the hundreds of thousands, or maybe billions, and they aren't all the same.

But I think just because our world can be perfect, that doesn't mean it is.

45

The second attack was swift. Of course, we saw them coming. Smelled, tasted, felt, and heard. It was the Banjxa and Ecdda again, in larger numbers. This time there were Dilidi with them as well. Not ones we'd met. But ones we'd observed—if I need to be more precise—which added cruelty, sarcasm, revulsion, and bravado. The Dilidi had seen us, and they'd snickered. Yes, this too, they thought. This looks like fun.

There are few actual borders in the ocean. There are no demarcations or straight lines. But there is the gradual pressure that mounts as you descend, and the cliffs you meet that slowly lead to an abyss. That's where we were now. Somewhere none of us had ever imagined reaching, where no one had ever wanted to go. Where the chemistry was also different.

When there's too much of a mineral in the water, it comes out of solution. Suddenly it sticks to your skin, and you can see it. But it hasn't been created. It was always there, in the ocean. It was busy, lurking.

When you died and I kept swimming down, Gola saved me. If not by the fins, then in ways that worked better. Perhaps in ways that gave him a better hold. Sometimes I imagine you. I see you. You're swimming beside me, and I have to forget your body no longer exists. Not even particles of it now. I open my mouth, but there is none of you. I've lost your taste. I've lost your smell. Then it is the same with my eyes.

Too far. Too deep. Too ethereal. Too long.

The first time the Banjxa and Ecdda attacked, they came at our nests. They carried bills and bones in their teeth. It was a show of dominance. It was violence and butchery, but above all it was a show. Of contempt. Would it have happened if I hadn't found the creature? No, because there was no reason for us to come together—not in the enormity of this world. We had our own lives, our own ways of doing things. We left each other alone. Instead, the creature brought us together and then it broke us apart. It brought us scorn.

This time the Banjxa, Ecdda, and Dilidi came for all of us. They did that together, too. It was after a third octopus had been killed, but I think there might have been more. There is never a righteous side in these kinds of battles, just as there are never sides in the ocean. The world is a sphere. We are responsible for all those who live in it, just as we are responsible for ourselves.

Would the Dilidi gamble on how many octopuses there actually were? Those numbers are also hard to count. Gjila says, Do not fight for honor or vengeance. Do not fight for causes. But, yes, fight for sport. The Dilidi didn't need another reason. When you fight, be prepared to kill. Fight and kill for ends.

When you consider the creatures in the ocean, we're each very different on the outside—the corals, the wrasses, the sharks, whales, and crabs, and us—but aren't we all made of the same things? The same sodium, calcium, sulfur, magnesium, phosphorous, and potassium? The world is vast, but our world is finite. As we tell one another, there's no place else to go. Unless we try to scramble onto land and see how long we can survive.

46

We went to the Caavaju. We went to Clova. There wasn't much to tell him that he didn't know. Sound and smell travel far, and quickly. Not unlike vibrations and repercussions. It had been the same with the Dilidi, and look where that experience left us. Clova clustered with his soldiers, but of course they'd had time to strategize before we arrived. He let us speak. He treated us with great respect. He offered sardines and kelp. He spoke of our common beginnings, when we were all one tribe in some forgotten cave. Then he answered, "If we were in your place, we'd have raced to us, too. But none of this had to happen. This mess, this wrath. These provocations. So we've decided we'll keep our distance. It's inevitable the tribes will fight one another now, and there may be a good amount of killing. The blood will be nice. But afterward you'll realize you need someone to lead you, and that can be us."

Unity. This would be the first time our tribes had joined together since we'd wandered apart. Never mind the reasons.

"It will be something we can all look forward to," Clova added. "But for now, have more fish."

The Ecdda like to be around blood in the water—it keeps their stomachs full and senses alert. If the Dilidi are hedonists, they like hysteria, too. We say the Banjxa move too quickly to think things out fully. The Caavaju just like themselves. But these alliances were dissolution. They were violence and menace. It was like swimming through red tide: you could taste and smell the pungency at your lips and on your skin. But this wasn't fear. We saw what our tribes were becoming, what all of us were, and it made us sick.

If you combine the ocean chemicals in ways they haven't mixed before, you'll end up with something new. You just need a catalyst. Something to sink or fall.

And then to spread.

I remember you, and us, and the family we were going to have. I could see them inside of you when you became translucent. They darted in every direction. I wonder how far they would have traveled. As they grow, they swim faster. But that was a different ocean.

This ocean feels empty. I can smell that difference now.

If there were any more of you left, I would eat it. Even after I lost you, you gave me strength.

With as few of the creatures as there must be on land, they must know what it's like to be alone. I wonder if some of them want it.

47

We picture it on land. Hot air blowing past it as it crawls across the rocks and sand. It grips a shell in its clingers, and then uses it to dig for whatever it can digest. It can't be the only creature, the only species. There must be fish flopping beside it, thrusting their gills into pools of water—maybe it eats the seals and whales it finds dead onshore, burrowing into their decomposing flesh like a cookiecutter shark. There are scuttling things alongside it. Lobsters, crabs, spiders. Twisting things. Slugs, eels, snakes. Flying things. Mobula rays, birds, flying fish. Somewhere there are plants that don't mind living in the open air.

Some have wandered toward the cold to escape the heat. They live on ice. They bury themselves inside it, freezing themselves inside carved-out chunks so they will barely age, their muscles so atrophied by the time they reach adolescence that there's no way out. They use the rocks and shells on land for that digging too, until their muscles are gone and they also are plants, just like the sea squirts that attach themselves to the corals and then start eating their own brains. Then the birds nip at them, if there's a thaw. The creatures watch them coming, swooping toward them through the sky, until the birds finally snatch their eyes.

A few head into the mountains, the terrestrial counterparts of our ocean trenches. They go to escape. They do not like it too hot or cold, so this is another choice. But mostly they go there so they can see the water from afar and dream about it and watch it roll, and wonder if they can return to this place where they must have once belonged, before whatever cruel joke nature played on them occurred and they lost every faculty they'd need to survive.

Perhaps they have their own stories. If you lose your stories, you lose circulation and you go numb. So they must keep retelling them to anyone who will listen.

I don't know if there are other minerals that exist outside of the water. But if there aren't, then they're made of the same stuff as us.

We still have the body, aside from the gonads and the detached limb that Brola took. We store it inside a cave on the edge of the canyon, not far from where I found it. It's begun to decompose and rise. You can see the bubbles leaking from the lesions on its skin. If it were anything else, we'd already have consumed the body whole, and if we hadn't, there's an entire ocean around us of hungry life.

The roof of the cave keeps it from floating away. It bounces against it. When we first pushed it inside, eddies got behind it and they'd force the body out. It would twist and tear, even as its lower limbs and nostrils caught on a few overhangs. So we used the limbs to push some shells and rocks toward the entrance. Their flattened ends made them especially useful, although this exerted pressure on the rest of the body, especially at the sockets where the limbs join the lower half. But eventually we built a wall, with the body trapped inside. That's where it is now. You can peer through holes in the formation and see it drifting back and forth, pressed up against the roof until a tiny current takes it and spins it around.

We've had to make sure scavengers don't get inside, or the rest of it would be gone in an instant. But, of course, they do. They are scavengers, and they are wily.

48

They were just bands that attacked. Mobs. They didn't represent entire tribes. We kept telling ourselves this every time there was an incursion. We went back to Clova. This time he held on to his sardines and kelp. "Those gangs will still be needed at the end," he told us. "Ours and the ones from other tribes. So I'm not going to say anything to them now. But you're right, it's shameful what they're doing. And unnecessary. We'll make sure they're better disciplined after this unpleasantness turns into war and we rely on them for help, once we start leading you."

Two of Clova's captains had switched genders since our last visit, which had been only days before. It's hard to know if they do this for themselves or to unnerve you. I could smell the change in hormones, the sweetness they spilled into the water, but there wasn't time for their bodies to have shrunk. The new female soldiers sized us up. We did the same. They had the look of mothers who would go berserk protecting their fry and wanted us to know it. They brushed past us with their anal fins. They didn't need to show their teeth, but both of them did.

We went to Brola. His troops turned us away, swam around us in tightening circles until we had to retreat, and then kept swimming around us as we did. We went to Doloca* of the Dilidi, the only one

*Do'lō'ca'kl'ēza.

143

among them who passes for a chief, mostly because he never tells any of the others what to do. "Come back when you're wounded, because that will be entertaining for us," he snorted. There was no one to try among the Ecdda. They're a shifting mass. Chaos. I won't call them a school.

So we attacked. The Ecdda are fierce but given to rage where strategy would be more useful. They're weaker without their sharks. We'd back them into caves and then come at them until they were trapped inside, just like our creature, with additional Gjala swarming behind us in defense. We didn't wall the Ecdda up, but we'd wound them and then let the scavengers in, the ones drawn to the taste of blood. We picked them off, one by one. Then the barracuda and trevally picked at their wounds, in throngs.

And we went to the Akla. The ones we knew the least and who seemed the most methodical and enigmatic of us all.

49

If you go back far enough, before there was Ooo or any other octopus, before we existed even as a glimmering speck, before there were fish or corals, eternity was an open ocean. Then life began. Single-celled organisms. Protozoa. Ciliates. Flagellates. Amoebas oozing through the water like specks of jelly. They drifted, fed, turned from one to two to four to nine or ten, and then to the larger numbers that are too chaotic and amorphous to calculate.

They organized themselves. They built. They built themselves. Until they had fins and snouts and gills and livers and hearts and blood. They acquired mouths and teeth and bones. They built themselves up into bodies. And then they built themselves into schools.

They turned themselves into many creatures. They became the coelacanths and the rays, the sharks and jacks and nudibranchs and mackerel and gobies and tuna and parrotfish and pufferfish and razorfish and viperfish and dolphins, and also us. Until the ocean was more than a shifting microbial mat, and everywhere it was alive. The corals weren't the only ones to build. We all had to do that to be here.

Whatever you think about numbers, there will always be ones that are too swollen and shapeless to fit inside your head, or that bounce around from one side of it to the other. The brain isn't infinite. Neither is the skull. Not even in the blue whales, where you sometimes have to swim around them, and then purposely ram theirs with your own to get their attention.

The single cells started conglomerating. At first, they must have drifted off from one another, swept by the currents into the enormity of the world around them. There's power in having endless space to roam—but even more in having a brawny tail and fins and a snapping jaw, and, practically speaking, you could roam through the same space that way, too. So they built themselves into everything around us. Everything living. It's hard to know if that was luck, determination, continued effort, or some godly design. But whichever it was, most of those advances were made without a brain. The fin and tail appeared over time. You didn't will them. But once they were there, you knew how to use them.

It's easier moving rocks. You can sweep them with your tail or nudge them into place with your fin or snout. It's not precise, but it doesn't require a lot of time or evolution. Basically, you just get behind and push. But the discovery of the creature's limbs changed our thinking and the process. It showed us you could build a frame to protect a design (for a while), or a wall to trap an Ecdda (until it died). Just as creatures grew from an agglomeration of cells, structures could be made from an agglomeration of shells and rocks. You just needed to put the pieces together and jumble them around until you had what you wanted. The cliffs and ridges were the result of slow geological forces, but you didn't have to wait for those. There were ways to speed things up. We don't have grasping forelimbs like the creature, capable of so much precision, but imagine what you could do if you had many. You could have eight like an octopus. Or you could gather together four land creatures and more or less achieve the same results. But if you amassed an army, the number of limbs would grow with each one you added, until they operated like a fearsome creature. Then who wouldn't want to enslave them? They'd just have to be obedient enough to learn to school.

50

That was how the Akla put it.

The fighting continued in our waters. It was inevitable that we'd come to them next—there was no place left for us to go. If our tribes have diverged from one another over time, nowhere do you see and feel it more than among the Akla. The scarification of their males when they come of age is only the start. Of course they look different. But they smell just like us.

We could see they'd recently completed the rite. Several male youths were covered in scalloped or striated scabs, while others flaunted their half-healed marks, swimming around us with their chests bulging like puffers just to show them off. Females of the same age ululated and clicked from a short distance away, but weren't as practiced as the older ones you usually hear. They all smelled young.

The older ones flittered in a camp, a depression on the ocean floor that allowed them to sweep herds of sea cucumbers up against its sides. Every so often an Akla would swoop down from above and grab one of them for a snack. As they bit, viscid fluid would gush out, which they'd slurp from the water before it began to dissipate.

We approached. The scabby youths weren't far from our tails, with their cheerleaders just behind them. Everyone needs a purpose. You go out and find one, if your world doesn't press one upon you first.

I took the lead, passing above the cucumber herds until we reached the center of their camp, where the Akla could approach from all sides and surround us. Gjila and I would have no swift way out, and we knew they'd know we knew it. That was the point. It was a display of deference. The ululations and clicking increased. We waited for them to die out, but they didn't. They wouldn't. They wanted us to know we'd need to talk above them. No niceties would be granted. The Caavaju had offered sardines and kelp, and look where that got us. But touch one of their cucumbers, and all teeth would be bared. That much was clear. Perhaps that was a start.

"I don't have to tell you about the fighting," I said into the water.

"You don't eat the octopuses after you kill them," one of them answered. "You could begin by telling us about that."

Amid the clicking and ululating, it was impossible to tell where the speaker's voice was coming from.

I finned forward without knowing if it was in the right direction. I wanted to exert myself. Perhaps how we presented ourselves would matter to them most. "Those were only a few occurrences," I began. "Committed by our young. They were angry. Helpless. Which is new for any of us to feel. That's not an excuse, but it's not why we're here."

"Octopuses aren't good to herd. They're much too smart. You can herd them once their arms are removed, as long as you eat them before they grow back. But you'd need to be a monster to do that. Is that what the Gjala are?"

"We came to talk about an alliance. Between our tribes."

"You didn't answer."

"You know the answer. We've come to discuss joining together."

"Why?"

"Because, like I said, you know about the fighting." I finned forward again, trying a new direction.

"We know that no one is fighting with us."

"The fighting will grow worse. It will spread. Everything spreads in the ocean."

"You talk like this is our first time in these waters. And yet here you are, in our camp."

The clicking kept growing louder, until it was a single indivisible thrum, a drone that came from all directions, one that no one in our own tribe made. Each new click filled the gap between the others. The Akla youth were equally adept, because it was all of the Akla who were making the noise together.

I raised my voice. "I mean you no disrespect. Nor does Gjila." But it was clear I'd underestimated them. The female adolescents had demonstrated that with their determination and cohesion. And maybe Gjila had too, because he'd let me go on uninterrupted, when both of us saw I wasn't getting through. Nevertheless, I continued: "The waters are different now. They're changing. If we could detect this in any of our usual ways, we'd all agree. We can observe the ocean—the shifts in temperature, the currents, storms, the minerals, schools, and the health of the herds. Like your delicious one of cucumbers. We can even sense emotion, what that does to you inside your body, and how you might react. But we can't detect words until they occur. Or attacks."

I tried to listen, to see if they were listening. The thrumming continued.

"We all remember when the seas were cooler," I continued, too. "When the corals were healthier. We thought we knew everything about this world, but maybe that isn't true. Some say that's the surface sadness. And its poison. We've always preferred the deep, where we thought nothing on land would affect us. But there are chasms here. Trenches that plunge the length of a thousand whales into the planet. And widening ones, where we can also disappear. So I'll be honest. We've never liked one another. Our tribes have kept apart. We haven't mixed. We haven't needed to. That's our sadness, too."

The thrumming abated just enough for a single response to come through: "If a Gjala mates with an Akla, we'll kill you all." There was a pause. "But if a Gjala courts an Akla, we will only kill him or her."

Now Gjila pushed forward. "Would you kill that Akla, too?"

"Don't be silly," the voice responded. "No Akla would ever want to mate with one of you."

"Then you have nothing to worry about," Gjila answered.

"The Gjala kill octopuses. Everyone knows that across the ocean. That worries us very much. That depravity. That monstrosity. But you've come to talk about fighting, and that's supposed to worry us less?"

"No," I answered, "it should worry you more, because the fighting will become a wave and you will see it, and it will kill Akla, Gjala, Banjxa, Caavaju, Dilidi, Ecdda, and Fantaskla, too."

"And also some octopuses, we suppose. So you'd like us to join you in starting that killing now. To team with you? And not just to tell ancient stories and sing. Although you can tell we're quite good at singing." By now, the thrumming had picked up volume, surging against my fins and skin, and pressing relentlessly into our heads. Had the walls of the circle the Akla made around us grown closer, too?

51

They had. The circle had slowly been constricting around us as our talk, or whatever it was, progressed. The droning had masked the Akla movements, and the speaker hadn't used any of our language's positional inflections to indicate they were approaching. Now the Akla were nearly upon us on all sides, and hovering above us, too.

"Show them you're unbothered," Gjila whispered to me, as we felt tails flicking above our heads. "Let them know you're pleased they've come closer."

I looked back at him quickly. "Give me more minerals than *that*."

"Lead."

The droning was louder now, but I knew that meant I wouldn't need to raise my own voice as much. Because of their proximity, the Akla wouldn't be able to hide where the speaker's voice was coming from. I watched her emerge from a wall of bodies, approaching me until we were nearly touching. The last time I'd been this close to another female was with you.

I could feel her smelling me now.

She was the only one of them who wasn't clicking.

"I know some tribes wonder what the Akla mothers do when their children are being scarred," she said, as she nodded toward one of their scabby youth. "Whether we look away, and whether we can't wait for it to be over."

She tasted the water sweeping across my skin.

"What do you think we do?"

"You watch."

"Only *watch*?"

"You tell your children the rite will turn them into adults. That the discomfort will recede."

"No, we tell them to remember the pain of each cut. The feel of the rocks and shells tearing across their skin. And gouging it. And we tell them to keep that memory with them when they go into battle, so that they know what they can endure. And also what hurts the most."

"That's it?"

She tasted, and swallowed again.

"But that once they're healed, they'll remember that not all touches hurt. And that's when they'll know who they are."

"The Gjala also know that not all touches hurt."

"But do you always know which one to expect?" She sniffed my skin. "Do you know which one to expect from me now?"

I didn't think she'd reach for me. Not in front of so many of her tribe, and not in front of Gjila. If she did, she knew I'd have to respond, and there wasn't any point in instigating a fight, which would be to submission. And then well beyond it. We hadn't come for that. That's not why the Akla had allowed us in.

The circle separated for us to swim through. So we didn't.

She knew that Gjila and I saw the way out, and also that we didn't take it.

Then she asked, "Is it true the creature's limb unfurls at its end like an anemone and can grasp a rock? Next time you come here, bring it with you."

Another one of the Akla pushed forward from the wall, holding a snapper-sized prickly skin sea cucumber in its mouth. Was this meant as a trade?

"No," I said. "If you want to see it, you'll have to come to us."

She clicked briefly, in a way that displayed her teeth.

Then she said, "My name is Aaa."*

---

* ʿAʾaˊaˊaaˊaa.

52

When we left, Aaa swam with us, too. Not in any real sense, but she was with me. She'd breathed and tasted me. I'd swallowed and smelled and tasted her, too. Gjila and I barely spoke, but we knew we'd made headway. It took four days for us to reach our waters. Home.

Once we arrived, I took as much of it into me as I could, until the waters had washed through my entire body, replacing the minerals I'd absorbed as we'd traveled, and I was different. Maybe closer to who I'd been before. The farther you venture, the more you change. You can't help it. It's as much a change when you're back, and that has nothing to do with the thoughts you have or things you see, because those reshape you, too. At once, you become both old and new. I was hungry. I caught a tuna, a bluefin, and feasted on its fatty gills and belly, before working my way up its sides to its back and then to its head. I devoured the fins, the eyes, the heart. The brains and cheeks and lips. Feasting, but also watching myself in the act, as if it were the first time I'd had those things in my mouth and I was surprised by how they tasted. Once I was done, there was only the skeleton left. A few eels and batfish looked on, hoping for any remains, wary of one another. But there was nothing besides the bones. Then I slept.

So I dreamed, I dreamed of you. Of the creature, of shoals of cucumbers, and of an ocean thick with fish. I dreamed of you still alive before the sharks, of legions of creatures scuttling on land, and of uncountable and infinite quantities of every animal that was delicious below it in the water, and even of fields of kelp. The world was full. I was full. My head was full. But it couldn't stay that way forever. I dreamed of Gola.

When I was young, learning about our tribes, he told us the secret was to remember we were all the same. We had the same fears and needs and mistrusts, but that isn't why we came together. It's why we stayed apart. If there were an Ooo, with all its limbs attached to the same body, it wouldn't survive by fighting with itself. A tentacle would attack. Another would lose. One might grow back, if the injury to the body hadn't been too severe. But too many lacerations would be fatal. And all that fighting wouldn't leave time for eating or defense against anyone else. So how do you tell yourself to get along with yourself? The idea of that is silly, so it's easier to tell parts of yourself to go away. I never dreamed Gola would, though. And I dreamed of you.

Before the sharks, after the quickened heartbeats, once we'd become a pair and our skin belonged to us both, and we'd begun curling up together in our nest when night swept over us like a welcomed tide . . . *back then*. Back then, you said, "I want more of us. I want little *us*es. I want them swimming across us, in our mouths, in our food, hoarding the best parts of our nest so there's no place left for us to go. I want them interrupting the things we say, the thoughts we have, and every moment of our peace until our peace is transformed into something new. Can I want that? Can you want that, too? Is that too much to ask? I want them to grow up then and swim away, even if that means we'll miss them. That's what I want to build for us. That kind of loss."

53

Neither of us dreamed of the particular kind of loss that came our way. But I've never been this particular creature dreaming of this particular loss before.

Each day, I'm new.

54

The land creatures' limbs, so suitable for use as tools, must keep them thinking about building and destroying, the various things they can make or break. Either way, it's about modifying their environment. It's easy to understand why they wouldn't like it as it is. To be castaways on those inhospitable, dry, and crumbling specks, coursing with whatever red tide is their own. Who wouldn't want to build a wall for protection? They'd need to build them into the sky to defend against tsunamis, unless their red tide wasn't in the water and it traveled through the air.

I wouldn't trust the open air with my life. The chlorines and chlorides in the water keep the ocean safe—and the viscousness of the water slows the projectiles from volcanoes. At least, that's how it used to be. But the more you're focused on moving nearby rocks, the less time there is for considering other things. Once we talked about other subjects, before we were in this mess.

Is that where we were sinking now? Just because we're big enough to make walls and other shapes doesn't mean that's all there is. Most of the ocean life doesn't have consciousness, and it's foolish to think there's any correlation between consciousness and physical size. The lion's mane jellyfish is larger than a blue whale, but you're not going to have a conversation with it. It doesn't even have a mouth.

We kiss and speak and bite and eat, and some of our neighbors brood their offspring in their mouths, giving up on eating until they mature. The mouth is the height of evolution, the focal point of the face. Sure, eyes are great. But you can live without them. There are lots of blind bathypelagic species, and you don't hear any of them complain.

So what about the creature's limbs? It's not that those would have made it vapid or single-minded, but you can see how they'd be a distraction. Dolphin males will sometimes coil a writhing eel around their parts for pleasure, or mount a headless fish. The females will rub themselves against the ocean floor. The land creatures must have masturbated ceaselessly with those dexterous forelimbs. I hope they didn't spout off about that as well. In the ocean, there are always impressionable fry around. I don't know if there are as many in its world, but we try to keep that stuff from them for the first few moon cycles.

To have limbs like that, you'd need a lot of self-control.

Or would they have needed someone to control them? That's what Aaa meant. (I later found out it was Aaa who'd said it.) It was a repulsive idea to think of using them as slaves, as if there could ever be slaves in the ocean. Unless that's what they wanted.

Not everyone in the uncountable schools wants to lead. But no one asks the creatures in the schools to do very much, except to stay with the group and help with its defense by adding size and complexity to its masses. Maybe then it's enough to be a follower. You show your face and your brawn, and let someone else do the thinking. You deny any personal responsibility. You make some noise through your mouth, when that seems useful.

But this idea was different. Maybe it was even a different kind of idea. It was convincing others to do the things that you wanted. No, that's not it. It was *making* them do it. Forcing them, or requiring them—depending on the individual. Either way, the goal was the same. Obedience.

Is that what having those limbs entailed? If how we get along together is what lets us survive in this world, would those limbs doom you to needing to be controlled? Who would decide? And if everyone in their world is like that, who controls the ones at the top?

You can't have everyone building what they want wherever they want to, and masturbating in between.

55

We are all a wave. We move tranquilly through the ocean. We aren't dangerous until the ground gets in the way. So what are you supposed to do, ask the wave to stop? Or the barrier to crumble?

Here's a rival theory: maybe it's not the presence of the limbs themselves (they grow from your body on their own, so it's not as if you will them to emerge, like a jawfish popping its head from the sand), but the creativity they bring out. We have creativity in the ways we love, in the ways we feel, in our thoughts. The limbs just help with expression in a different way. There's the creativity of destruction, and that other kind that builds.

Aaa arrived with an entourage. Closer to the surface, the tropicals would say a half-moon had passed since Gjila and I had made our visit. But at our depths, we gauge time by the currents, by how many things they bring or take away. Usually what that tells you is more important.

Ever since I'd found the land creature, it felt as though time had stopped. But it's also what started it moving again for me after you died, even if I was only substituting one body for another, one that was also coming apart.

There were more Akla than we could count, perhaps as many as the total number of clingers on the creature's remaining limbs (you see why counting is complicated). We felt them approaching through the water—the sweep of their tails and trimming of their fins—but they came without making any clicks or ululations.

The first utterance, then, was Aaa's:

"Show us."

There were three youths in the group, their ragged scars still bright. They inflated their chests.

"You saw the creature after I found it," I answered her softly. "All the tribes came here, including yours."

"You showed us that it was strange, not strangely wonderful. And also maybe useful."

"Not all the Gjala trust you."

"They shouldn't. We don't trust you. But that's a start. Just be sure that what I warned you about mating with Akla is understood by everyone in your tribe, because I wouldn't want the retribution to be surprising."

That's how we became friends. Or allies, really. She instructed the youths to wait by the perimeter of our camp, and we brought the remaining members of her group to the cave where Gjila had stored the body. We showed them the wall we'd constructed to trap it inside, and the Akla watched as we took it down. You didn't need to destroy it. You could just disassemble the stones and shells, place them nearby in the sand, and then know they'd be there in the same uncountable quantity when you put them back. Maybe that should have been obvious, but we'd never had to do that before. And why would we? Would someone now need to compose a song about building, dismantling, and reassembling a wall so that we wouldn't forget? Songs are memory. We are all dimwits in silent seas.

We tugged the body out, careful to keep it from brushing up against the cave's sides any more than it had to. Each time we did, we'd lose some of the skin and gristle to the currents. We saw a few brittle stars and fish had gotten through the wall and nibbled what they could. We wouldn't have the body forever—that much was clear. Except maybe for the bones. And that would only be if we could keep the zombie worms at a distance. Their females secrete an acid from their skin that dissolves skeletons, so they can gobble the trapped fats and proteins up, while a hundred minuscule males live inside their bodies. Males like that give all of us a bad name.

We showed Aaa the limb, the one we still had that had detached from its upper body and was floating freely in the cave, like a broken piece of knobby sea rod coral. You could see where Gjila had held it in his mouth, the indentations in the muscles and skin that each tooth had made.

I demonstrated how the opposite end opened and closed, the nimble motions that it was capable of, the ways we imagined the land creature had used it—or once had used the pair. We even built part of the wall up again, using its forelimb as a tool to grab the stones and shells and then deposit them in the preferred place, which turned out to be a complicated maneuver. Yes, we could have done this with our teeth, until our snouts got in the way.

"I'm not going to say anything more about having them as slaves, because this is the only one, and it's dead," Aaa said. "But we would have had a lot to teach it. It would have found our world a very hospitable place."

"Except for the fighting. And the killing. And the retribution."

"Except for those."

But the creature had things to show us too, and the fact that we didn't discuss this any more was proof that it was on both of our minds.

56

Just because we were going to be allies, it didn't mean we'd start with trust. Once Aaa left, we moved the body to a different cave and piled the stones until the barrier was twice as thick.

Gjila had come across some of our youths tearing at an octopus's arms, and he'd attacked them so ferociously that he said he'd forgotten how good it felt to fight. He trounced them, and left them huddled and bleeding. Then he said, "Do not swim away."

He waited for their blood to enter the current, for other creatures to be able to taste this.

"Do you think that scares the Banjxa?" he asked them. "Do you think mutilating an octopus will make them less likely to want to attack? Do you think if they did . . . what you've done would make any of us want to come to your defense?"

"We can't do . . . *nothing*."

Gjila told me that once he felt the bloodlust well up inside him, he had to remind himself to stop attacking. It was like the sharks' feeding frenzy. A head full of electric eels.

"Don't be fooled into thinking there's ever nothing. Not anymore than saying the ocean is empty." He showed his teeth. "Unless you want to be a part of that nothingness now."

The problem with fear as a motivating factor is it only works as long as others are afraid, and you can never tell when they'll start feeling brave, bored, or stupid. At best, it can be a temporary measure, but it will never keep a hungry creature from trying to eat. Or an angry one from biting back. You have to give that creature a chance for food, or at least for hope. You need to act.

"Wouldn't you rather be part of an army?"

Banjxa swimmers hide in the mid-ocean ridges, ones barely perceptible against the flatness and wideness of the deep ocean basin, and there's no way to sense them until they come jetting out.

The Ecdda swarm, but we fight them into the caves. The Caavaju and Dilidi watch, pretending they're uninterested—until there's a moment to strike and then, afterward, to deny it. But no one gets the upper fin. It is ebb and flow. It is a storm of eddies. It is currents you can predict but wish would never come.

Remind me how we got here?

57

It starts with love. It's how we occupy ourselves when we aren't feeding or mating. We want more. We always do. It's normal to be dissatisfied, no matter how many fry you have or sardines there are to eat. You could have a particularly comfy nest with a sprawling ocean view, but it's not about possessions. It's simply wanting more. So we invent love. We do it so everything we feel we feel profoundly, and that makes everything we do seem more important. The other tribes say we're single-minded about this, but don't they want more too—indulgence, entertainment, adulation, creation stories, violence, speed? How do you convince yourself to want less? And what is less in a world without possessions? Unless it's teaching yourself to regress and lose consciousness, until you can't remember how to feel.

I don't know if the land creatures have belongings, but what are you if there's no place where you belong?

When we met, I wanted to belong more than anything else. To the ocean, to myself, and especially to you. I knew the three of them were connected. I was already a part of the ocean. If I wasn't part of it, I wasn't part of any place in the world. I already had myself. And yet there was a void, in an ocean that was solid liquid fullness.

How can the ocean not be enough?

What else is there? The wretched emptiness of land, where only plants and birds launch into the void?

Not everyone needs a mate. Not everyone needs to mate—or they need to mate, but they don't need a thousand children. I can't say you were the half of me that was missing and then I found it, because that's nonsense. There are many possible mates, including incompatible ones. But I can say that after you were gone, and after our children were, half of me was missing, too. Or maybe it was more than half.

Is there any way to count how much it was? To give it an amount? A number?

58

The creature had ten clingers. If you count them, that doesn't change. They don't float off or swim away.

Each limb ends with five. If you add all four limbs together, they come to twenty, even if the ones on the lower limbs are smaller. You could easily expect them to equal more, but they don't. Sure, sometimes you get a different number when you start with one and then keep adding more, but I've come to realize the actual number is always the same. Counting isn't always reliable, which is what you'd expect. Math can be untrustworthy, but it is also splendid magic.

And then there's more: you can have a number and end up with a smaller one when you take some away. Whatever it is you're counting at the moment. It doesn't have to be clingers. It could be starfish, or how much you feel. That's how you quantify loss.

Having you made me a twenty, but now I'm six.

I'll teach that to the Akla, because it works with sea cucumbers, too.

59

Maybe you could plan things out. We know the currents, we know where it's going to be especially salty or cold, the length of gestation for a thousand species, where we are in relation to each other by the positional inflections we use, the depth of the trenches, and when the tuna will present themselves to us as feasts. We know when the coral will spawn and where to find the best vantage point to watch (and then where to go afterward for some privacy of your own). The male white-spotted pufferfish, who builds elaborate nests in the sand to attract his mate, must know what his creation is going to look and feel like before he starts. The same for the corkwing wrasse, who builds his orb-shaped nests using seaweed, stones, and mucus. And perhaps a little hope.

So maybe you could plan ahead how many rocks or shells you were going to line up in the sand, counting them out in small but reliable quantities, before you changed direction and then made a new row, possibly at an angle. And then another. You could do this over and over, and soon you'd have a formula for it so you didn't need to feel the knowledge was inside you and instinctual, but something you had learned, and the idea of whatever you made would still be there after the lighter shells had washed away, or after a squad of Banjxa had come to destroy it, and then couldn't understand why you barely put up a fight or how what you'd made could reappear so quickly once they left. Like magic. Again and again.

One day, you could also make something big.

The Akla mark themselves. Even more than their ululations and clicking, it is their identifying feature, since it's possible for the females to stay quiet—but not for their males to cover their chests. The tradition is as old as any of us can remember. It is part of all our legends. And yet the Akla don't discuss it much, other than to say it is a rite of passage, performed when their males turn four.

Our tribes keep their distance from one another. Our world is large and rich, and every shellful of water is impossibly bountiful and complex, not even considering the mollusks living inside.

I can't figure out the meaning of the Akla clicks. It's as if they speak a second language besides the one the rest of us share. That's a queer idea, since the goal of language has always been to communicate with others. Sure, our pronunciations, grammar, and vocabulary differ from tribe to tribe. We have different names for some of the organisms around us, which sometimes gets confusing, but those organisms also have different characteristics in different parts of the ocean, so that actually makes sense.

I've understood that the scarification of the males' chests is not arbitrary. The marks are not identical—how could they ever be?— and yet they are the same. I don't mean they repeat: we don't even have words for what I mean. The Akla use the same cuts to make patterns that belong together, as if they're part of a single family. The markings match, like the different shapes and stripes on blue-spot, spot-tail, and black-backed butterflyfish, but they are more than pictures. They mean something. But nothing they resemble.

~~~

"Mark yourselves," the Akla tell us. They come in groups and talk at us from all directions. "Use the edges of scallop shells, and we'll tell you how deep and where to cut. Then you'll have markings on you, just like we do. They won't be the same, because our males do it when they're young. You'll do it when you're older, and your females will do it, too. It won't look as good, but it will mean we're united."

"What will the markings mean?"

"Like I said, that we are together."

"No. What will they mean exactly? Will they be the same ones that you have on you?"

"Why would you want those? Those are for us."

"Show us what you mean with shells in the sand. Then we'll decide if we want to do it."

"If you don't, it will mean we are apart."

60

It was a crazy idea. So was it any crazier that the youths who'd attacked the octopuses now wanted to team up with the Akla? Sure, some of them joined Gjila's army, but not all. There is an inevitability to discoveries. Everything that is in the world already exists. So we're pulled to them, as we are into an eddy. Not just to what we find around us, but to what's in ourselves.

Droves of youths wanted the marks. They couldn't understand why none of us had thought of making them before, when the Akla had been doing this all along. You didn't need a scallop shell, just anything that was sharp. They marked themselves indiscriminately. Some of the gashes looked bungled. Some looked horrid, crazy. They swam to the Akla like that, propelling themselves toward them as fast as they could, to keep the nematodes and copepods out of their cuts.

61

Their marks were gibberish, like the thoughts that occupied their minds and pushed the sensible ones away. We raise our young. We think we're doing it right. And then it turns to this.

How do you decide who deserves the blame? Who gets to assign it?

Before the land creature was found, we thought we lived in a hermetic world—ocean all around us, and the vacant sky far above, with only birds who fished the surface and the shallows. The water sealed itself as soon as they left. But then the land creature came, and it tumbled down and sank to us, and its discovery brought ideas that covered it like a film and seeped from its body, and I don't know why we expected them to be wonderful.

The Akla studied the Gjala youth who arrived and asked them what their patterns meant.

"Nothing? Like empty words?" the Akla clicked. "Then why did you do it?"

62

Sharks tear the smaller fish into bits, flooding the clear midnight blue with blood. Then other fish come, hoping to swallow whatever the sharks leave behind without getting swallowed up themselves. Not everyone will be a winner.

The Ecdda swarm amid the sharks, who serve as a distraction. Occasionally, they'll grab a small fish themselves, as an energy booster. They're the only ones who eat while they attack. It's unsettling to watch. They'll keep attacking with a tail hanging out of their mouths.

Egg eaters are the lowest caste of carnivores, but they ask if it isn't crueler to eat an animal who has already been born. Butterflyfish will wait until the nests of damselfish are unguarded to swoop down for their eggs. They explain it saves the parents the anguish of having to watch, but obviously that's an excuse. Despite their garish colors, the butterflyfish are useful for plotting attacks on collaborators. They flit around lethally, like sprays of lava.

You can seize an enemy before you kill it and force it to eat parasitic worms, so the worms attach themselves to its gut, anchoring themselves by the spiny hooks on their proboscises. No matter how much your enemy eats, it will starve to death. You can feed it more as amusement. But this rarely serves a purpose, unless your goal is to brainwash it.

Are our Gjala brainwashed, the ones cutting at their own skin? Sometimes I think that's the only explanation that makes any sense.

Are there rules for fighting your own kind? I don't mean when you engage, but how you do it, how you kill? Usually, we go for the heart to end it quickly, but attacking the stomach is effective, too. That's how I lost you.

Now we also chase our kind into caves.

I don't understand more about the Akla's marks, except that there's a method to them, and the males are fiercely proud of those marks on their chests, and the females are proud of them too, even while their skin stays untouched.

"What do they mean?" I've asked Aaa.

"They are messages," she answers. Ones you only get a single chance to send, even if that chance lasts your entire life. Better you don't get it wrong.

"Why don't the females have them, too?"

"We are likelier to change our minds, and we do other things with our bellies and chests."

Our females are stones and shells that have many ways to fit together, and to come apart.

63

"Show me how it works."

"These are the marks I'd make." She traced the edge of the broken shell across my chest, holding it between her teeth. I felt her face by me—rivulets streaming from her mouth around the shell, washing across the pattern where she had almost cut through my skin.

"What does it mean?"

She released the shell and let it fall. "Aaa."

I watched it tumble and nestle in the sand.

Then she said, "You'd wear that on you. My name. For life. On your chest. All the Akla would recognize it, but your Gjala wouldn't know what it means."

She looked at me. Her gaze was like a school of blue chromis flitting back and forth across the reef, a phosphorescent gash in the ocean, across my body, and through it, too.

"Of course, that would be too many of us for you to count it as a secret."

64

"The Gjala would know if we told them. Or if you did." That's how she put it. As though it were information you'd distribute like food. "Other Gjala could also wear those marks, but I think you'd want them for yourself."

The Akla had begun showing the Gjala youth how to make the patterns, devising whatever came into their minds, and then cutting into them with little thought. It was embarrassing. Were they incising other Akla names, as if they belonged to them like property? Or was it more a stream of consciousness—your shell becomes your body, which becomes the ocean. You watch it move wherever it goes and look for meaning in it afterward. If there is no meaning, you make it up.

We told the Gjala youth to stop, but they were defiant. Yes, we are creatures of love, but I didn't love those Gjala personally. They were the ones who had attacked the octopuses, but then hadn't joined Gjila's army. I felt no sympathy for them, but I was chagrined by how this reflected on all of us. We told the Akla to stop. They looked at us with disbelief. They said, "Do you want to fight with us, too?"

I asked Aaa. She said, "Your Gjala consent. Are you asking us to control them? Isn't that what the Caavaju said you needed? Maybe they were right."

The attacks continued. Banjxa appeared from nowhere, decimating nests with sweeps of their tails, but also with rocks and bones in their mouths, using them to break and bash. A few searched for the land creature, but their attacks seemed so arbitrary and savage that finding it in its cave wouldn't have stopped them. Perhaps the Banjxa weren't so different from the butterflyfish with their blitzes. They lacked the fancy colors, but they made up for them with heft and speed. The Ecdda and their sharks simply overwhelmed our smaller bands with gnashing waves of teeth. We had to warn our weaker and younger Gjala not to venture from our camps, except in schools—although it's true our schools were especially susceptible to attacks. They're an easy target for anyone who wants the attention.

The Banjxa and Ecdda weren't alone. Dilidi and Caavaju attacked as well. They had a new strategy. Once, we'd had everything we needed. Then war brings innovation. The Caavaju would arrive from above, too close to the sunlight zone for us to recognize their presence, lugging boulders from the ocean floor, ones it would have taken three or more of them to carry. Except that they arrived by the hundreds. Then they would let them drop. Those boulders plummeted through the water columns, demolishing anything underneath. Once, not long ago, only edible bits slipped through the currents. Manna. Now there was this. And smaller stones fell, too. Those were meant to be ironic, an insult and a nuisance. That was how the Dilidi liked to do it, sniggering.

Gjila's army would attack, but it wasn't large enough to defend our families and their nests. It couldn't hope to strike the other tribes in their camps to preempt their campaigns. We couldn't survive alone.

Or we *could* survive, but not as we were.

Gola would have had advice. I don't know if Gjila was depleted, but he fought valiantly and spread his energy and commitment among his troops. It poured out to them, even to those who had behaved shamefully in the past. Some would position themselves so they were down-current from him, and the water would wash over him before it reached their bodies.

"I could urinate, and they'd like it," he said with a sigh. "But I won't."

Gola would have.

65

I sniff the waters for Gola, but there's nothing there. He fled. Had he stayed, he'd probably be dead. He wouldn't have been agile enough as a swimmer to evade the attacks. And yet I feel betrayed. He left. Did you feel the same toward me when the sharks came at you? Did you wonder where I was? And if I'd fled?

I sniff for you, but there's nothing. There can't be, and I know it. But that doesn't stop me, because each sniff is hope, and it means there's a split second each time before I register your absence, and all those split seconds together make me feel delirious, like I'm hyperventilating. It's just a self-indulgent lie. I know that. There's no possibility that you remain because I know what happened to your body, the feel of it in my throat and the feel of you in my stomach. The surge of energy in me afterward. I just can't think about how you felt. The things I imagine that went through your head, before your thoughts dissolved, and then your head was apart.

Did you smell the waters for me as the sharks approached? Was there any hope amid the teeth? Hope plus pain is still pain, but maybe it's accompanied by a little less sorrow.

I don't know what goes through Gjila's soldiers' minds as they fight, or what they smell in the water besides the determination and strength of their captain, the *hali'kā*. But maybe that also gives them hope. And resolve. Maybe Gjila has a few minerals left inside him yet. There's comfort in knowing that if they die, their comrades will eat what remains. Unless the sharks get to it first, and their blood makes them go berserk.

A mark. A small one. In an obvious place, but without any obvious meaning. Not so different from the fishes. No one asks them what theirs mean.

Maybe it's not exactly the same. The Akla would know. Aaa would know. And so would I. And somehow so would you. That's the part of it I imagine. The parts of you I can't detect in the water that would know and still be able to smell and taste it. The parts that would hear and feel how the currents run differently across my skin now, as I swim.

66

Do the land creatures mark themselves? Would they mark the skin of others? Would you do this to control them, debase them, or, like the Akla, would they say this is something they want? Do they think their bodies are too plain? The splendid dottyback would never think that. Or the regal angelfish. Or the psychedelic wrasse. Does that mean our bodies are missing something? Our females become translucent when aroused. Isn't that enough?

"Who said the mark would be small? I have a name. It's not a secret. You would wear it on your chest. Others would see it and call you by my name, too. Aaa. Would you like that? No, you don't have to answer. You can't answer now. You haven't imagined it yet. Imagine it first. Not the pain—that part is unavoidable. But how it will be afterward, when you wake up from it and it's the first thing you see and then everything floods back to you, and you remember. Would you like that? I would like that. For you, I mean. Everything to be forever. Nothing disappearing. Or washing away. Yes, I also turn translucent. I'm turning translucent now. You can see into me. Aaa."

67

They came as red tide, furious, incessant, deadly, thick. The tribes we'd once thought of as part of us, and now were only adversaries, enemies, killers. They made us into our own red tide, too. We spilled into the currents.

Bite off a head and drag the body down, and pressure squeezes the fluids out. Then the snappers and stingrays come to feed.

There has to be a response. When you lose someone, you can't just swallow your reactions, plus whatever is left. But there has to be another way to feel alive without someone next to you, or inside you, having to die. If you start to think the others around you seem especially energetic, it might be time to reconsider where you've finished up yourself.

I remember when I was small, I used to swim with my eyes closed. Did the land creature scuttle around like that, too? Until you're swallowed whole or bitten in half, there is joy to innocence. The ocean is a colorful place if you choose to go where there is color, and gloominess if you head for depth and cold and murk. Each flick of your tail is a choice of direction. That's why they take up a third of our bodies. One-third is free will. The rest is history, biology, facts, and momentum.

I went back to Aaa. To the Akla. Past the outliers who inhabit the peripheries of the craters, and their adolescents who still look and sound like innocents themselves. They know me now and what we've lost. I'd like to think they sang to me, but the Caavaju would have liked to think they sang to them, too.

I swam above Gjala youth, the ones who were covering themselves with Akla markings without any sense for what they meant. I don't know what was in their minds as they watched me pass them, like a distant fish. Way back when, our tribes had gathered along the canyon's edge, and we'd addressed one another nervously, excitedly, and cautiously. The world was an open ocean. It was ours. When you speak, sound isn't the only thing that comes from your mouth. There are also vibrations, warmth, minerals, and hope.

Then you close your mouth, and if not to tear at flesh or to swallow, it is a time for quiet. A different kind of pregnant hope. Open it again, and there's a vacuum. Everyone can sense it. Even those who don't have words. No one has ever proved that creatures who can't speak actually want to. I think they see speaking as unstoppable flatulence, and they are embarrassed in its presence.

I swam. Beneath me, the Gjala became fewer and fewer, and the Akla numbers thickened. They twisted around glinting formations in the sand, and I watched them making more, depositing fragments of stones and shells on the ocean floor with the crunching of their teeth.

68

The shapes looked random and mostly sat flat against the sand. They'd been built in clusters, seven or eight together. The Akla twirled among them, but differently around each set. At one, the males spun wide circles around the stones until they reached the spot where they'd begun, before launching new circles in the opposite direction. At another, Akla had gathered food—lobsters, prawns, sea cucumbers, and snappers they'd killed and pinned down with rocks. At a third, a trickle of Akla girls approached as languorously as eels and then swam off in exactly the same pattern. Then they reappeared singing, spat stones and shells from their mouths, and started constructing more shapes of their own.

I sensed Aaa behind me.

"What is it?" I asked her.

"Everything that matters."

I listened to them click, the incessant stream of pops and crackles, like the claws of snapping shrimp. When the shells were still in their mouths, the Akla girls snapped pairs of them together, creating clicks from that, too. But they didn't hold on to any. They continued making more patterns in the sand.

They clicked as they worked, darting off and back, while the males kept forging circles, and every once in a while a new female arrived to spit more stones and shells into the larder. Soon the females had built a trail, as long as the tentacles of a man-of-war.

"Do you like it?" Aaa asked, as I felt her cut into me.

The shell entered my chest, and then continued deeper. The Akla males had expanded their circles, until they were wide enough that Aaa and I floated inside them.

"This is when the sharks come," she told me softly. "It's best to be prepared."

The males swam around us now, forming a wall.

I could smell and taste my blood entering the water, and the pain joining both sensations in the current, as though that pain had weight and movement, too. Aaa continued to carve, and I could feel the mucus tear, as my skin and a layer of muscle split, the filaments unraveling and flooding with blood.

"You'll feel me when you move. Your muscles will have my name."

The shell bit down. This was the closest I'd come to knowing how it felt to be eaten alive.

"'A'a'ā'aa'aa," she repeated, cutting.

The sharks arrived, as expected. The Ecdda weren't far behind.

69

The sharks charged the circle, but they couldn't penetrate it. With the males swimming in rings, there wasn't a lasting gap to attack. When the Akla changed direction, it confused the sharks even more. They're predators, not tacticians. They do what they have always done.

The sharks tried again and again, because that is what they also do.

We watched them from inside, a kaleidoscopic array of spinning rings, of dashing Akla, charging sharks, roiling water—the flashing twisting flanks of fish, and the roving glinting chains of their teeth. Occasionally, the view grew hazy with the ooze of my drifting and coagulating blood.

Aaa carved. "This matters, too," she said. "This tradition. These marks. My name." She let up just a little. "But maybe now not as much."

Ecdda soldiers tried to breach the ring, but they also were unable. They swam fast and hard, and then were either churned up by the whirling band of Akla males or they bounced away, ricocheting into open water or against the rocks. Then the adolescent females pounced. They swarmed the dazed Ecdda and began to click and scream. Their ululations were like the dolphins' percussive blasts—a cacophony of pulses, booms, and cracks that broke their focus and maybe their minds, too. I hadn't heard them make those sounds before.

When they weren't screaming, they bit. And tore.

Aaa moved us to one side, and the ring changed directions, parting briefly to let three sharks enter. Then it switched directions again, and this time one of the dazed Ecdda was nudged into its interior. The kaleidoscope continued—flanks and ripples and fins and teeth—but now there was new blood inside it. The sharks had new prey, and the single stupefied and wounded Ecdda had no way of fighting back. They devoured him. And then the next Ecdda. And the one after that. The Akla kept at this until no more Ecdda remained, and then they turned their attention to the sharks and watched them prey on one another until only a single one of them was left. It was satiated and sluggish now, and it would remember what it had done, and also the taste of Ecdda meat.

They let it swim back to wherever it considered home.

The Akla feasted too until there was nothing left to consume inside their ring, and then they disbanded.

The pain at my chest had begun to subside, as Aaa moved toward my flanks. "Why do these marks matter less to you now?" I asked her.

"Because there are more of them."

"Then you didn't need to do this?"

"We need to do everything we can."

70

I knew some of the Gjala had watched the ring. None of us had ever seen anything like it before. The land creature's dexterity had inspired us to trap Ecdda soldiers inside caves by piling up stones, but the Akla defense and counterattack was more coordinated and refined than anything we'd conceived. Even more, it was something the Akla had done before and practiced. Something with a protocol.

It was the same for the pattern on my chest and flanks. All the Gjala in the Akla camps bore markings, and now that also was true for me. The patterns shamed me. And yet they were essential. And yet they hardly mattered to the Akla anymore. Or perhaps just to Aaa. Whose name was forever carved into my skin, my memory, and my muscles.

The Gjala in the camp nodded to me, and I felt only contempt. And yet this is what I'd come there for.

If I was going to lead, was I supposed to convince the rest of the Gjala they needed markings, too? Was I supposed to hold these Gjala up as my example?

When you're ready to abandon everything and forsake what you know and have always kept by your heart, only then can you become invincible. That's when the skin that holds you together tears, and you can assume a new form. The immortal jellyfish, nudibranchs, rockmovers, and flatfish know this as they transform from earlier stages. Now I knew this, too. My skin was off. Aaa had already torn mine.

Every creature that's born from an egg knows there's a moment of suddenness, of dawn, when you ooze your way outside into a larger stranger life, but when we grow up swimming freely that's easy to forget.

When we sensed each other from across the ocean, would you have wondered about the marks on me? I didn't have them yet— but would you have known they'd develop later? If we all know we're going to die, that means we can predict the future. We have that knowledge, and then we ignore it. Instead, we look around for lunch.

Maybe the Gjala here deserved a kinder thought. They under-stood our future. And they knew what was necessary for all of us to be in it.

71

Another ring. A dead Gjala inside, one of Gjila's soldiers. More sharks, more Ecdda, and now also some Caavaju. An impenetrable circle. Gjila's soldiers fought the attackers first. As soon as one of them died, the Akla arrived en masse. Was the Gjala bait? Certainly, one of them was. Gjila knew that. I won't ask him to discuss it. You don't go to war thinking you'll have a total victory, but maybe you go to war not completely thinking.

The Gjala bled. Sharks don't need more than a drop, but this one provided copious amounts. He flooded the water, and the sharks couldn't resist. They came from oceans away, but it took the Akla only a few seconds to slip into formation, and for their ring to start spinning around the injured Gjala. The sharks charged and charged. The Ecdda and Caavaju spurred them on. And while they did, our Gjala soldiers attacked from every side. New rings formed around our wounded each time one of them was hurt, but not around the Ecdda or Caavaju. Once they were the more accessible prey, the sharks turned on them, and the Akla girls cheered them on.

72

I sing a song to the blood-drenched sea. A song of victory and of loss, of gain and sorrow, of life and death. I sing with the Akla, clicking along silently in my throat. I sing for the fallen Gjala, today's and tomorrow's. I sing of construction and creation. I sing of walls.

I sing of the Ecdda and the Caavaju, the transformation of their bodies into spoils. I sing of that last moment when they were alive, their awareness of what they would become, and especially their experience of it.

I sing of the Dilidi, of their fattened egos, and how tasty they will also be to the sharks.

I sing of the Akla patterns in the sand, the Akla circles made of flesh, and the Akla booms and screeches. I sing of the blood-red tide.

I sing of Gola.

I sing of the markings on my skin.

I sing of our armies. I sing of the land creature. I sing of what we've learned.

I sing of loss. I sing of protest.

Once, I sang to you.

I was happier singing songs of love. And also hearing them.

Think of the Akla rings as eddies. Eddies with cores of teeth. Like other eddies, they can last for seconds, months, or years. They nourish themselves as long as they keep being fed.

The Banjxa came next, swimming faster and gaining speed. We could feel them approach, the water they displaced and the reverberations of their wakes. We could hear and sense and taste them. And then we could see them charging, because it would take our eyes to appreciate their contempt. They came. How many more Akla swimming together would the circles need to withstand them? How many abreast?

I've already admitted we have trouble counting that high.

But the correct answer turns out to be zero. The circle changed directions, cued by several quick Akla clicks, parting suddenly to let the Banjxa through and then parting a second time as they exited the opposite side.

I was right about the Dilidi and the succulence of their egos. I saw the careening Banjxa smash them into rocks—the Dilidi bruising, bleeding, bursting—as the sharks gleefully converged on their battered forms, before they knew what had hit them.

73

Brola watched the attack. He didn't charge himself. He swam in wide circles of his own. He lurked and studied, and then he swam off.

He's less dangerous when he speaks or sings, but the Akla were the only ones who were making any sounds. Unless you count the gnashing and crunching of the sharks, and the squeals and hisses of gases escaping from the Dilidi bodies. Because then it was cacophony.

Could you make a war song out of that? Has there ever been a composition with so many musical parts?

The remaining Dilidi could dance to that, to the sounds they made themselves.

I sing a song to the violence of creation, to our new world, the one that's changed around us more than the oceans ever have, to the shriveled shapes of land, and to the new shapes that have started forming below, made of thoughts and shells and stones.

Then the Banjxa attacked again.

This time, their mouths were full. They swam at the Akla rings—mechanisms as precisely timed as coral spawns—and then spat out broken corals and giant clams, bones, rocks, full skeletons, kelp. Some of those floated, some hovered. Others sank or tangled. The

Akla hit them and careened, their bodies knocking into one another and tumbling, out of control.

Yes, the Banjxa mouths also came equipped with teeth.

We didn't give it a name. None of us did, because naming it would have been too awful. Instead, it became that *thing*. That event. The situation that necessarily changed ours. An alteration in the current.

We couldn't count the dead, but the Akla said it was four hundred and thirty-eight. Somehow, they believed it was that number exactly. I don't know how it would have been different if it had been more or fewer. I knew some of the Akla who had died. Their faces, voices, and smells. Their heartbeats and the radiance of their bioelectro-magnetic fields. The relationships and fry left behind. But also now how they tasted together, the combination of their bodies, their blood, their bones and flesh, and the way you could have two or twenty subtly different textures and flavors in your mouth at once, and how that would be something new, calamitous, and pleasant.

That also didn't have a name.

We don't talk about our dead, other than the ones we've loved. We talk about mates, children, siblings, parents, grandparents, and great-grandparents—but not about the generations who came before them, except for vaguely. That's what makes mythology possible. It introduces error, doubt, and infinite ways to reinvent our story. We certainly could have been a single tribe once, but drifting apart from one another as Ooo's severed tentacles is a stretch.

74

The Akla laid out stones, one for each of the dead, large enough that the currents wouldn't move them, wouldn't dare. They placed them in a pattern. Some of the Akla came with food and left it beside the markers. When the currents washed over them, the offerings formed little eddies.

During the attacks, Gjila's soldiers had moved the body to a closer cave, one that was less than a day away, to protect it. Now Gjila retrieved the body and placed it among the stones.

All he said was, "Enough."

Everything that enters the water becomes a part of it eventually. The land creature was already dissolving. It was always going to do that, without any help from us. All that clicking in the past, but now none of the Akla spoke. And none of us said anything either. The ocean is thick, and fluid, and full, and if you add something new to it, it has no choice but to swell. Almost as if you had struck it.

You could gaze at the eddies and think of them as swirls of life—even if all that life, and death, was also inside us, nourishing and strengthening us, and enraging us, too. The stones the Akla laid out were memories. If you counted them slowly, they added up to a number. But they also had a meaning, because they were the warriors we had lost.

"No, they're more," Aaa said, breaking her silence, "but we haven't started singing it yet."

75

You could count them. Do it over and over, in any direction. You could stop midway and then continue without it having any effect. You could stop to hunt or mate or sleep, and then pick up the following day and still get the same number. The unspeakable question was whether the Akla would form another ring, the Banjxa would attack, and if there'd be so many more dead, and so many rocks and shells and sorrow and bones, that you could scientifically test this again.

76

'Amā'a'akl'shlw'rēre 'agā ra'rēre niru hōlla xla'hōlla xla'shlw'rēle yc.
'Amā'a'akl'shlw'rēre ezla eza kl'avaj yc. O'o'ō'xla'hōlla. Brol'usll'rēre.
Glo'vynī'ēz 'ahōlla 'a hā'ique kāstla. 'Akl'shlw'rēre, 'ayī'ki'kīya. Ezla
eza niruv'hōlla glo'vy ēz xla'a'niru rēre gjal'ra 'aa'aa niru yc. Brol'xhōlla
kl'ezda. 'Agā'ra. Cla'vā'shlw'rēre hōlla xla'hōlla yc. Shlw'el'a. Gjalā'niru
shlw'el'a yc. 'Amā'a'akal'shlw'rēre te'cla va'cla'va'hōlla ezla eza 'aa'aa
niru. 'Agā'ra uxma'hōlla. Uxma'avaj. Glo'yvnī'ēz fla'ela'dwa' omi'dwa
uxma'avā xla'shlw. Banj'xhōlla 'amā'a'akal. Banj'xhōlla 'amā'qma'ēz.
Ec'dda'kl'ēz 'amā'a'akal. Ec'dda'kl'ēz 'amā'qma'ēz. Ca'avaj'u'usll
'amā'a'akal. Ca'avaj'u'usll 'amā'qma'ēz. Dilidillil 'amā'a'akal. Dilidillil
'amā'qma'ēz. Gjalā'niru shlw'el'a. Niru'xlu'cla't usll'xlu'cla't. Gji'vnī'ēz
te'cla ka'nāstla ka'nācla 'av'cla'xlu hōlla niru na'ura bl'oxla oxla'fa'cla.
Uxma'avaj. 'Agā'ra. Shlw'julu'ulu' oma'ēz va'cl'va'hōlla xla'hōlla.
'Amā'a'akal'shlw'rēre 'agā'ra'rēre niru hōlla xla'hōlla xla'shlw'rēle yc.
Amā'a'akal'shlw'rēre ezla eza kl'avaj. O'o'ō'xla'hōlla. Brol'usll'rēre.
Glo'vynī'ēz hōlla 'a hā'ique kāstla. 'Akl'shlw'rēre, 'ayī'ki'kīya. Ezla eza
niruv'hōlla glo'vy ēz xla'a'niru rēre gjal'ra 'aa'aa niru. Kātla'ca'kla
gjalā'onu. Kātla'ca'kla gjalā'onu. O'miga'rēre kl'ido'o. O'miga'rēre
kl'emdo'okla calla. Finuklā'imoto yc, finuk'idolo yc, finuk'imoro yc,
finuk'ixlāzo yc. 'Agā'ra. 'Agā'ra dan niru hōlla. 'Agā'ra dan niru xla'hōlla
xla'shlw'rēle. Finuklā'imoto, finuk'idolo, finuk'imoro, finuk'ixlāzo.
O'o'ō'xla'hōlla. Uxma'avaj. Uxma'avaj'alla klo. Eza, eza, qma'ēz. Eza,
eza, qma'ēz.

77

The song went on for two days and nights, repeating like a series of waves, crashing down around us. As the Akla sang, they laid more stones on the oozy floor, creating a pattern that was larger than anything I'd seen or imagined could exist. It eclipsed the ribs and caudal fin in our Gjala canyon. The markings covered an area so broad they stretched beyond the edges of the Akla craters, and then spilled like sound into the nearly infinite distance. I suppose you could try to count the stones, but what really mattered was their sequence. You only had to swim above them. Then they resembled a field of coral—the sprawling kind we barely see anymore, with branches emerging from larger stalks that cleaved into newer and smaller ones, again and again—but still, they were more complex. Nature does what it makes sense for nature to do. We do what we can conceive.

I recognized some of the shapes from that first Akla field, when I first encountered the Akla rings and their warriors had seemed invincible as they churned the Ecdda into pieces. Those marking weren't so different from the ones I'd seen on their adolescent males or that were now crudely and blindly copied onto our Gjala skin. Now they were an ocean. One of patterns and shapes. A song.

I wondered if I swam above it enough times, back and forth and up and down, and let it imprint on my brain, whether I could start to sing it, too.

What would you think of this world of ours and everything it has become? A place of peace and undulations and embracing currents that somehow has turned into this? I'll remember it as a place of love, because that is my memory and it is my right. If there were a change to the chemical composition of the water, we'd have been able to smell it. The sharks can taste a single drop of blood amid a million parts of water, but all we hear them talk about is how good the Ecdda taste and how unfair it is they didn't eat any of them until now.

I sniff at the water, wanting solid facts. But here they disintegrate and then dissolve. The only certainty you can have about anything is how they were for one split second. And also, how you feel, because no one can tell you that you are wrong, although they will try.

78

Gjila returned to our camp to expand our army, like a bubble rising.

I swam across the sprawl. Aaa watched me. I could sense her at a distance. She darted away each time I looked, but she had to know I'd seen her. We have many ways of apprehending the environment. Sometimes the best thing about eyes is just their taste.

Instead, I felt her. I felt her vibrations in the water. I felt the percussions of her heart. I felt her smell and tang. I felt her heat. Every once in a while, I caught a glimpse of her fluttering tail. And, yes, I felt her name carved into my skin.

If you looked at me from above, you'd have said I blended in with the stones, each time I twisted onto my back. I was markings over markings, camouflaged among their shapes. If the patterns below me had a meaning, maybe I was changing that now. I'd be their meaning, too. If you could see me.

You'd have to sense me.

I was retribution, remorse, violence, nostalgia, loss. I was sure swift motion, threading through openings and around boulders. I was sleight of fin and reprisal, sorrow. I was myth, history, and conviction. I was all our fry, both living and the dead. I was Gola and Gjila, and Galla and Govili. I was you, as I've always been. But could you tell I was also Aaa, or would you need your eyes for that?

~~~

We swam in circles, massive rings thicker than any the Akla had made before. I was part of them now, along with other Gjala. We were six and seven thick. The Banjxa would race into us and send those on the outsides of our circles tumbling, but the interior rings would hold. Slowly our rings crawled forward, like a gargantuan crown-of-thorns starfish devouring coral. Where the terrain dipped, we'd pivot slightly on an axis, skimming the ocean floor with our chests and then arching through the blue-tinged black, an Akla or Gjala mouth following each hammering tail, with a frantic heart chasing just behind it. Woe to the cucumbers and grunts that got in our way. We churned them up and turned them into sand.

We followed the shapes as they spread out from the Akla craters into the ocean, in the direction of the territories of the other tribes. We were a song of death, our rings a whirl of creation and destruction, a monster in the sea, a gyre of insatiable bodies.

We were the tentacles of Ooo, spiraling out from the center. We were unfurled rage, a tumult of bodies held together by song, the cohesiveness of notes that wrapped around us like a strengthening fiber. The song would push us forward.

We were coming for the Banjxa first.

79

Was Ooo the Banjxa's creator, or was it the other way around? The Banjxa came up with their ur-octopus story, and we added the epilogue of mutilation and slaughter. I preferred the Akla composition to our own. As we followed the path of stones and shells toward the Banjxa camp, at least theirs had direction. We could sing of love as much as we liked, but most love ballads are about desire, while war songs focus on taking action.

We spiraled through the abyss, tumbling forward. The grunts and cucumbers were the least of it. We tore up beds of clams, flattened seamounts, and left scars across the ridges. We kept to our ring, a juggernaut through the open ocean. The remoras detached, then disappeared. The spider crabs fled.

Has there ever been anything as formidable as a giant ring spinning forward across the ocean floor? The land creature would have stared in awe. He would not have been able to imagine it. You make these things in order to destroy, because no other motive would make any sense. You could hear and feel us rumble. You could smell the rage in us, too.

We covered leagues, feeding as we swam. We'd open our mouths and swallow plankton as we hurtled forward, somersaulting like mantas. Even with our jaws clenched, we could filter the plankton through our teeth. We swam for days. We were too deep for there to be a night, but we could feel the tug and gush of the tides, while they streamed back and forth, far above our heads, against the terror of the open air. In that undeveloped realm, you couldn't understand problems like ours. The land creatures wouldn't war among themselves, as we were doing now, because none of them would have anything the others would want.

In the ocean, however, it was glorious. We swam even while we slept. The centripetal force of our ring helped keep us together, but we hardly needed to be awake. We can swim in our sleep, although most of us know not to do it, since there is no way to evade predators or to navigate. But we took turns staying alert. We were our own sentries. And we rumbled forward.

The ocean floor transformed as we crossed it, from sand to mud to ooze to rocks to abyss. We were a hovering ring, a constellation, while the ocean trenches gaped far beneath us, and we twirled above them like delicate ctenophores, imperceptible in the immensity. But we were also death. That was our purpose. We'd ravage, kill. Let Ooo come, not the little octopuses, and we'd take care of him, too.

Come to us, Father. Show us the way into your heart.

Then the rocks and cliffs fell away. The floor grew shallower. Banks of deepwater corals appeared, massifs of them that tapered into forests and then into groves. We were approaching the Banjxa habitat now, all of us awake and all of us fed—a few from our ring had broken away to hunt and then feed us mackerel and sardines on the move, because now the plankton would not be enough—and we were back in formation. We swam. We spun. We swarmed.

And then we entered an emptiness, that strange *da'nāhai* that wasn't supposed to exist. It was the first time I'd beheld anything like it. Where the corals ended, the ground had been laid to waste. You could see where once there had been nests. You could smell them.

We continued spinning. Above the pulverized corals and stones, we found ourselves amid desolation. We could have stopped swimming, but none of us dared. When sharks stop swimming, they begin to sink. For them, that danger is real. Everything around you makes an impression, but if you sink too far in the ocean, it can cut into you instead.

80

Residue was all that remained. Bones and rocks. Fragmented corals and shattered shells. The Banjxa had done this to themselves, to their own lairs. You could see where they'd taken shells and stones in their mouths and banged and gashed them against their nests, into the surrounding fields and against one another, until nothing was left that wouldn't soon be mud or sand. Maybe they sang a lamentation, or one of hate, but there was no way for us to know. We listened for the residue of a paean or a hymn, notes still embedded in the water like minerals, but there were none we could hear or taste. No vibrations. So much violence without a comment is the same as love expressed with indifference.

Then the Banjxa swam off, for nothing remained except for the savoriness of their skin and blood. Those particles lodge themselves in the nooks and cracks, but eventually they also float away.

81

We sniffed and sifted through the rubble. We used our tongues.

"We can't stay here," Aaa warned.

We'd broken from the ring, and we saw the other Akla and Gjala swimmers were struggling to stay in formation this close to the ocean floor without the ring moving forward. We hunt, and we turn ourselves into sharks, so desperate for a taste of blood that we can't control our bodies or our minds. We don't know if we'll sink or swim. All we want to do is attack.

I would remember this day, and maybe there'd be one when I would hate the sharks a little less. But I couldn't say that for the Banjxa.

Had they done this to themselves? There doesn't have to be an army that forces you from your home. You can turn yourself into an exile. You can swim off into the distance.

Maybe you'd have a reason.

There were hundreds of other Banjxa camps, maybe thousands. We wondered what had happened at them. Did they still exist? Had the same Banjxa attacked them? Maybe the families there had attacked themselves. There could be other options. But too many to count. Some you wouldn't want to.

Think of love. Think of creation. Think of existence. Think of the eight arms of Ooo—no, make them thirty—attacking one another, twisting around themselves like giant moray eels, squeezing and tearing. And then turning on their own limbless body, applying pressure, until Ooo, the great ur-octopus who is venerated as much as the water itself, erupted through its head. And then think of those detached limbs twisting around senselessly, disconnected from reality, brainless, and shriveling after that. Kill the mouth, and you can't feed yourself. Kill the brain, and you can't think that far ahead.

We listened again, as hard as we were able. Maybe there'd be a remaining sound trapped inside a shell or buried deep beneath the sand. There could even be one caught in an eddy and muted by its whirl. You can't whisper in the ocean. Press a conch to your head, and you hear the entire timeless sea. Sound travels too fast and far for subterfuge. We knew we'd hear voices if there were any, but we only heard our own.

Aaa was right. We couldn't stay. Not like this, open to an attack. So we rumbled forward. We stayed in formation. We kept our fins pressed close against our bodies and swam using only our tails.

82

I never believed in Ooo, but I wanted to now. I wanted Ooo to be missed. So there wouldn't be a limit to what was gone from the world for any of us.

It took a full day to reach the next Banjxa camp. Maybe they could cover that distance in half the time, but we kept in formation in case one of their squads came at us. We swam through empty water. Increase the volume, and it's still *da'nāhai*. That is spatial physics, biochemistry, ontology, math. Every breath is magnetism and minerals, smells and tastes and life, but something had changed to the ecosystem, something fundamental. Now the entire expanse was a void, and only the presence of other swimmers—friends, companions, rescuers, Akla and Gjala alike—would keep the rest of us plummeting through it. We live at depths that are suitable for our temperaments and our bodies. Below that, there is only sleep and chaos. And aside from our occasional forays, everything that lives in that world is oblivious to us. Maybe they think we are ghosts.

We found the same desolation at the second camp. Perhaps chaos isn't actually part of the ocean floor, because the quiet decimation there takes eons to occur, and what we encountered could just have easily happened overnight.

The camp was lifeless. Destruction has its own flavor. Dryness, exhaustion. Disappointment. Once there were great clusters of happy creatures living together. What creates this kind of devastation? Who gives it permission?

Who forgives it afterward, once enough time has passed?

This much violence is disease. Where is the feast that normally follows this much killing? Where is the territory you're protecting if you do this to yourself?

In the center of the camp, there was a crater. It was barely recognizable unless you hovered above it, since it was only a few snout lengths deep. But as you approached from the sides, the shells and stones inside it grew smaller and smaller, until the shards themselves had turned to pebbles and those, in turn, had turned to sand. A few goatfish were rifling through the crater's bottom with their barbels, searching for food (yes, even in death, there is always the hope for life). But the crater's center consisted of the finest grains, and there wasn't a single morsel among them. You could imagine how that center could be a nest, and how it would be the softest place to rest your body. You could imagine how rapturous it would feel to lie there with another and explore your partner's body and bring it pleasure—and to wrap around it and engulf it, and to feel that pleasure yourself. And then you could imagine a swarm of Banjxa pounding at the nests and dens that were inside that crater with rocks in their mouths and with their tails, and even striking at their young, until they'd pulverized everything that was there into this soft and welcoming bed, and everything that had once been alive inside it had been turned into powder.

Then as we swam above, a lone Banjxa appeared, went back to that banging, and all we could do was watch.

I broke formation and ventured down. He ignored me. I could have been an illusion, but he'd still have been able to sense and smell me, unless he thought those were illusions, too. He worked around me as if I were part of the seascape or a wave. He banged. He backed up so that he could generate speed, coiled his tail, and released, crashing headfirst into the sand with a Triton's trumpet shell clenched between his teeth. His face was bloodied, as was his mouth. His eyes looked everywhere but nowhere, except at that patch of sand on the floor before him. Again, he rammed into the crater. And again. You could see the bone in his jaw where his skin was torn, blood mixing into the water amid a puff of particles of sand. Even the sharks were smart enough to stay away. Only then he stopped.

"Cousin," he said dazedly, "I wonder if you've seen the nest that was here. Or if you can smell it. I keep digging . . . if it's broken into many pieces, then it should be easy to find one or two . . . once you smash them up, it should mean you're left with more . . . isn't that the math everybody's talking about now? . . . It's wonderful to see all the love your babies have when you give them a comfortable place to snuggle. It turns their faces so happy and ruddy . . . but I'm wasting time talking to you when there's still so much to do to get it ready . . . I don't know why you keep insisting . . . our world keeps getting richer and richer, but it still needs us to caress and care for it a little more. There can't be enough tenderness and love. Not for our babies. Do you hear them singing, the way they squeal? The softness of their flesh when it's inside your mouth, against your tongue?"

He let the Triton's trumpet shell drop to the ground, displaying a viscous sheen across his teeth.

83

We don't have a word in *yc* for "prisoner." Until we trapped the Eccda in the caves, we'd never forced another living creature into a confined space. You evade, you kill, or you kill and eat. Sometimes you threaten, often as a bluff. Normally, those are our choices.

But none of those was appropriate now. Evading the Banjxa soldier—were we even certain that's what he was?—was unnecessary, but there was something wrong with his mind. Was there a parasite inside it? The rest of him might still be edible and even tasty, but you'd be crazy to take that chance. *Crazy.* That's what he was. Infected. Sometimes you observe behavior you don't understand. I'm sorry we didn't get to see the land creature alive because that would have been fascinating, to see the things it did and the choices it made, as it scurried along the desiccated ground, desperately lapping at its urine. But other times you *do* understand behavior, like when one animal challenges another it can't possibly defeat, and you recognize that its decision to fight is so misguided that the only explanation is there's something wrong with its brain.

That's how it was with this particular Banjxa. We hadn't seen this kind of behavior before. You look around, you think and observe using all your senses, and then you act in a way that's rational, not obstinately believing in a world that doesn't exist—or that a single sense is so strong, or infallible, that it can crowd the others out. We could have killed him and let his body float away—but then he might have been eaten by other creatures, spreading the contagion. Or we could have ignored him, just as he'd first appeared to ignore me. But it was also possible we could learn something from him, and with Banjxa—even sick ones—you can't be sure you'll get another chance. So we took him with us as a prisoner. Seven in our circle (I think it was seven) broke away and formed their own ring around him, one he wouldn't be able to force his way through.

"Come with us," they told him.

"Are you taking me to the children? I already have so many of them inside my head . . . that's such a good place for me to put them."

We live in water, but somehow I had the image that the blood in his mouth wouldn't dissolve away.

We continued forward. A giant sphere, and a smaller one circling it, in an orbit. Some things do not exist in nature, but we had started inventing them now.

We headed back to the Akla camp. It would be a four-day journey. We tossed him scraps of fish we caught. He was giddy when he heard the singing at the camp's border. I've never understood if the Akla females sing all the time or just when there is something to say, like now. The Banjxa had given up trying to break through our ring, but those adolescent ululations set him off. He swam circles inside our own, frequently changing directions. If there had been more than one of him, he'd have attempted to school, but he was the lunatic. The loner.

Akla boys and girls watched the spectacle. Their numbers grew as more and more of them arrived, until they'd formed a shoal of their own inside the camp. Shoals are messy things, whether they're fish or *yc* gathered together. A mass of unruly creatures moving every which way, in a clump. But when they begin to school, united in the same direction, it becomes a movement. Then they're worth noticing, because you want to know what they'll do. Then you observe. Perhaps you spy. When our Gjala started marking themselves just as the Akla did, that was one. Same for when they took their rage out on the octopuses, as horrifying as that was.

The Banjxa attacks were a movement, whether they came at us or at themselves. So was making shapes in the sand with shells and stones. And once, before anyone can remember, an Akla marked his skin. Maybe that was the first.

You might think the ocean is all movement, but a lot of it is ebb and flow, and then it is just muddling around.

Was our prisoner a movement? Confining him, I mean. What if he wasn't crazy? Would we have done that to him then? No, we would have killed and eaten him, and taken pleasure in the succulence of his flesh. But maybe we also would have played with him, because sometimes it helps to tenderize the older ones first.

He was giddy seeing all the Akla children. We could taste his saliva mixing into the water.

84

A movement of limited movement. Call it that. We kept the Banjxa soldier contained. Every once in a while, if he tried to stray, an Akla would swim above and drop a boulder through the water column, confining him or pinning him down. Just as the Caavaju had taught us to do.

He seemed to enjoy this.

He regarded the stones as manna tumbling down to him from above, in giant chunks. So rich and varied is the world we live in. He'd snap at them hungrily. His mouth stayed bloody. If you added a few children to nibble on, he'd have everything he could ever need. Oh, what fun, the game!

The ocean courses and brings you everything. You only need a little patience.

"Children," he asked, as the Akla sang at him, "which ones of you are here for dinner? I like to plan out my meals."

85

Everything in the ocean comes with salt. How tasteless the food in the land creatures' world must be. The blandness and monotony of living there. Do they all eventually starve to death, once dissatisfaction overtakes them?

To live where there are no resources. To live where it is dry. Where there's not enough gravity or buoyancy—no neutrality, so that you can just float. They must all want something better, for themselves. For their kin. But does it exist? Maybe they dream about it. Fever dreams where there's no water to put them out, fantasies boiling inside their heads, turning their brains into sea urchins, the deliciousness that's just beneath the spines. Maybe it's the ones with the best imaginations who are able to stay alive, whose fantasies are sufficient.

And then the Akla adolescents attacked. It was bound to happen. Like I've said, the inevitability of what was in the current. They attacked with a song, a guttural riff of vengeance and hunger. Aaa tried to stop them, but her voice only joined theirs. It made it richer and filled the unwhisperable water. Until it was an uncontrollable torrent. The Banjxa soldier resisted, but there were too many mouths. When he saw he couldn't win, he changed allegiances and started eating himself. He was greedy about getting the choicest parts.

86

I had no appetite for him. I don't know if the Akla youth felt more cheated or repulsed when he began gorging on his own anatomy. It's hard to know at what point he lost consciousness, but it's reasonable to say that happened before we found him.

By the time we arrived, only his body was left.

It was a mystery why the Banjxa had destroyed their nests. But we weren't going to visit them all—as if somehow that had become our responsibility, even while their soldiers kept up their attacks. When you swim from your camp, you head into an abyss. It doesn't have to be deep. Chasms stretch in every direction. The whole ocean is our home, but it's not true that we know it. There are creatures in the depths with distensible stomachs that can accommodate your whole body and digest you while you're still alive. Or dazzle you with a lure until your flesh welcomes the serrations of their teeth. Or call you "cousin" or "brother" before taking your life. When you see these creatures, the idea that you come from the same place as they is nauseating. So you stop and sniff. You tell yourself to fin warily. Or else you decide that speed is the only way to a safer beyond, even if it is into the unknown. Maybe that's how Gola felt when he swam off. He just got there sooner.

I saw Aaa along the farthest edge of the throng, but she didn't say a word. She was speechless.

There was more devastation on the journey back to our Gjala camp. Aaa remained at her own camp to lead and protect it. Maybe the Banjxa had grown addicted to attacking, so when they ran out of adversaries they simply turned on themselves. Addicted. Just like the sharks, amid their sprawls of blood. The more there is, the more you want. You swim through it, and it becomes a part of you. You smell and taste it. You can't pretend it isn't there.

The Banjxa families in their camps would never have seen their soldiers coming. Never have imagined they'd attack.

This is how I imagine it: the Banjxa soldiers thought, why deny yourself something you enjoy for a single moment longer than you have to? We can feel our camps as we near them. The temptation just grows stronger.

We deny ourselves in love, teasing ourselves with frustration. Every sniff and swallow of ocean water isn't just a hint, but a promise of what awaits. That's what makes it delectable and something to prolong. Sometimes our males will wait weeks to culminate their acts of love, until the moment when their partners have turned into sponges and can only absorb them. But in battle, you strike when that striking is unexpected. And then you kill completely, because there is no coming back for more.

As they attacked, the Banjxa thought: this is easy, this is glorious, this is satisfying, this is fun. And they might have said: *I like. I like. I want this.* If they composed a song, it was a love song to the killing, and it drifted between the molecules. But like the sharks, they could detect every single particle, every note. The song would grow stronger with each camp they reached, until it swept across them like a current, and the only thing better than the memory of killing was killing again.

Maybe I'm making some of this up, but that doesn't mean I'm not right.

Sometimes things spread.

87

That's the song I sang on the journey back. The song that didn't exist, which I couldn't stop singing. A song of death.

Yes, once there were songs about other things. I sang of the ocean, of its tidal forces and warmth and breadth, the way it swept around you and embraced you, fed you, bathed you, brought you everything you needed, and took away what you didn't. It was all there was—the connectivity, the world, the past, the present, and the future—and the only thing the ocean didn't promise was love, although if you were lucky it would bring that to you, too. But then it was your job to keep it.

That ocean has disappeared, even if it's the same water. The whales don't sing to us anymore.

I don't want to sing about the future. Or the present. I think I'd be happy to live in the past even more than I already do. Go back. Go back, like the salmon. We all know where we come from. We can taste the minerals, feel the electromagnetic pull, differentiate between minuscule variations in temperatures, telegraph our position with changes in our grammar, and remember the topography of the ocean floor just as specifically as we can a face. But that was supposed to mean we also knew where we were heading.

Your face was a map. I don't have it anymore. I remember it and see it like an apparition pouring out of my veins, but I don't know how it would have changed. Across the years we should have had together. I only know the current took it away, particle by particle. It takes away everything that matters. And what doesn't matter, too.

We love the water and depend on it, but the water is indifferent. We give it everything, but we can't trust it.

Can the land creatures trust the earth and air? We've seen the earth collapse along its edges, skidding down the continental shelves and slopes. Then it becomes a part of you, and the air above us grows fetid and dark, but we're no experts in that realm.

Of course I wouldn't live there. I don't know anybody who would.

Here's a tale of love: a thousand babies swimming across your skin, bubbles gurgling from their gills. Or another: the ocean swirling with your taste and scent so that I'm with you even when I'm not, or with a hundred of you when we're together, because you're everywhere and I'm everywhere, and that's also a song because I don't know what else to call it.

Sink to me. Sink to me. Or I'll sink myself into the abyss, where it's quiet and nothing ever leaves.

Was I going home, or down? Does it matter? I was descending. We were thousands. And then came the attack, in all its finality and brutality. I'd witnessed the devastation the Banjxa soldiers had brought before, but this was Banjxa, Caavaju, and Ecdda all together. And maybe also Dilidi. It was a swarm. Not the way fish school in a mass, but how algae spreads, mindless and relentless, suffocating. That song. The Banjxa tore into us from the flanks, compressing us as we swam. Then we were as stretched out as a giant eel when the Caavaju assailed us from the front (or were we more like a sea cucumber, defenseless and only able to expel a little fluid from our anuses, along with our digestive tracts?), and the Ecdda came from behind, picking off our swimmers one by one. The moment when you're turning around is when you're especially susceptible to a strike. Or to many, which was how the Caavaju had organized their assault. Were there sharks? Now there didn't need to be. They set on us five against one. We're not good at math, but even we can figure that one out.

Our tribes had always lived apart. We knew one another, knew each tribe's territory, its habits, and its smell, but we kept our distance. Sometimes we passed one another in the open ocean, and sometimes we could sense each other's electromagnetic fields. But this was something else, something new. There were alliances now. Tribes working together. Sure, it sounded nice—but the goal was annihilation. Tribes teamed up to do that faster, in a frenzy of break, kill, pound. Like the waves, relentless.

And, yes, there were also sharks.

88

A sea of blood. Our own. As thick as squid ink. They let me live. They saw the markings on my chest.

So there'd be someone left to tell the story. Always one.

89

I watched them die. In the moments as I turned. In the split seconds, as the Ecdda launched into their flanks, some with their mouths agape, and others with sprays of stones they spat into the gashes. In the stoniness of the Banjxa eyes, as sharks attacked our swimmers' dorsal fins and tails, and their broken spines twisted outside of their skin. And in the blood, as it spread through the water—an ocean inundating ocean—so thick I couldn't separate the individual Gjala anymore.

Sinews and lost consciousness mixed as one.

I ate what I could, because anything less would have been obscene.

We are timeless, and yet there has to be a first. Even a first time the water moves a certain way. But does that mean there'll be a second, third, or fourth time, eddying into forever? Are there things that happen only once after they've been invented? I only loved you once. I only loved once at all, but I didn't invent the emotion. There was someone who had to be the first. We go on and on about our fantastical octopus, but not about that. If there's a first, does there also have to be a last?

I was the first and last to love you. That's *my* origin story.

We become creatures of action so we don't have to think. Just because we can, it doesn't mean it's worth the effort. Or the discomfort.

Or the pain. Did the Banjxa think? Did the Caavaju or the Ecdda in the moment they attacked? Or the Dilidi, as they lurked at a distance? Or had all of them stopped thinking by then?

We know the truth, but we swim past it. Out of fear that it will slow us down.

And who says love was the first emotion we felt? Maybe it was the last.

I swim past the heads. And the faces. Gjala and Akla heads tumbling through the water, severed from the bodies they were attached to, wriggling with hungry fish, a thousand tails twitching as they feed, so the heads look like giant sea urchins plummeting all around me, and the twitching tails are the only things that aren't oozing, and I can hear every one of them slapping back and forth, back and forth, pushing the water away.

90

Most of the time you try to take an inward look there's nothing you can see. So many butterflyfish have fake eyes on their flanks, but someone should try connecting a real one to a heart, where it could finally do some good.

Maybe the land creatures' eyes work differently. Or maybe they eat them when they start to fail. Once you eat the eyes, the sockets can be a good place to store some food.

The Banjxa, Caavaju, Ecdda, and Dilidi left me because of the markings on my chest, but they couldn't have thought I was an Akla, not up close. It would take a generation of living in their waters for me to smell like them. That's the only test. Not just to sing their songs, but to exude their stink.

Maybe the other tribes suspected how the markings could be used. To tell the stories of what we saw. To say the impossible. About what they had done. And to do it in a way that lasted longer than any of us. So there would be a messenger.

I sing a song of devastation. I wear it on my chest. It's a song of destruction. Of decimation.

I've seen everyone cascade around me. I chased after them for a closer look. At some point, we're all heaviness in the water. The currents take us. The ocean sweeps up its mess. Rocks rain through it. You can do anything with the rocks you can conceive of. You can write names in the sand.

It's a song of love. And commitment.

I've seen it with my eyes.

91

It would be a three-day swim back to our camp, more depending on the currents. I'd travel it alone, but no one would touch me. I was untouchable now. That doesn't mean I was protected.

To be touched in a way you don't want is to feel your whole body stiffen, and nothing in the ocean is like that, where everything is fluid, flexible, curved. Except for the pointiness of teeth. And the fractured edges of bones and stones. I was unmarked, except for the ones Aaa had scored into my skin.

It was a different ocean now. I coursed its seas, some of them so unchanged I thought they belonged to a foreign world. Pastures of rippling sand. Garden eels poking their heads out of them, like seagrass. Pelagic rays undulating past, as though they were unexpected currents themselves.

And yet, just beyond, there were bodies decomposing, shifting in the surge. Bloated heaps that every nearby creature would wriggle through and fill its belly on. And even those that don't have bellies. Sometimes it's easy to dream of a world without consciousness, but you'd need consciousness for that.

I passed ridges. I passed walls, ones that tumbled down to the ocean floor and into trenches, where all you have to do is sink beside them to watch the last evidence of life fade out.

I stopped. I ate. I went after good, clean food. Animals I could eat that weren't a way of cherishing the remains of our own. You kill, you eat. There's not supposed to be more of a story.

I passed more scenes of fighting. Of annihilation. Because that's what it was. Nests that had been built high, from stones and shells—not the little mounds that crabs sometimes push together, but ones tall enough to fit our bodies and even some of our kin. And then others that had been knocked down. More of those. Bloated heaps of those. Rubble nests. Rubble homes. It would be nice to think there was no life trapped inside, but when you see the scavengers approaching, you know that's not the case. You can smell and taste that life as you swim by, and sometimes even hear it. The feeding and the squealing. The scavengers eating, and others dying.

There's no way to save a life once half of it has already been digested.

If your eyes were positioned to look inside you, at least you'd be able to see which parts were gone.

I kept swimming, counting the surges and tides, and the trickles of light that made it this far down and signaled when it was day and night.

I swam through storms of the planet's making and the ones we had made ourselves. I swam through nothing. Open plains of empty water. *Da'nāhai.* It had never felt like that to me before.

I swam through memories. At least those were full. I shut my mouth tightly so none would spill out. But they do—then you have to snap at them before they drift away. Maybe that's what's in the mind of snapping sharks. They're after blood, but also the memory of it.

When I was a child, I dreamed of the ocean and everything there was inside it. I dreamed of its enormity. We drifted off into a sea of endless possibility, all of us did. But I never dreamed of this. Possibility had its limits. You could go anywhere then.

Is that true? We know the world isn't all water. Inside the planet's core, there is rock and fire. The creatures who live there seem to like it. They don't complain it's bleak, dark, and cold or burning hot. They don't go to live somewhere else. And far above us there is the air. The seals and whales and dolphins breathe it, and some of the fish leap to take in gulps, but it is poison. The life there is poison. The land creature's discovery is proof of that. He is poison to our world. Just imagine if we were poison to his.

Far above, the waves break and splash on the surface, straining to become the color of the sky. Sometimes we'll dare to go see them. But why surrender that blueness just to become infected white? The deep is the only sanctuary there can be. Far beyond our depths, our suffering sinks and fades away. Drag it there by the tail, and it compresses into nothingness. Both love and misery do. They slow down and constrict, while the foraminifera, amphipods, and polynoid worms blindly go about their business.

It was Gola who so long ago stopped me from sinking there. That also was after death. But now I was heading home. Long ago, home had already changed. And now it had changed again. The whole ocean has. Once there was light in the water. Now the trail of bones and skeletons points the way.

There's not just air above us, but also sun and moon and stars. I wonder if the air infects them, too. If there are currents above us, and the moon and stars have minds, why wouldn't they just whirl away? Yes, there are also birds in the world. They can't get enough of us.

I swam. I swam because that's what my body was designed to do. But it was also my responsibility. To see, to sing, to swim.

When you swallow and smell as you sing, your song reveals what's inside you. Then the ocean life knows who and what you are, while it listens. There is no hiding or pretending then, as there never was from you.

I smelled and heard and tasted you die. The same thing was happening to me now—all at once, and then again and again each time I passed a body. There is no stagnant water in the ocean. All of it mixes. News travels everywhere. I imagine the land creature scuttles everywhere, too.

I passed cliffs and fields, crags and slopes and open expanses. Sand covers everything in time. And everything becomes sand. Including songs.

Life passes. So does death. But both endure. As long as anyone remembers. The amphipods and foraminifera don't remember anything, but I have higher expectations for the rest of us.

The scents grew stronger as I approached our camp. The sea was redolent with the effervescence of Gjala lives. There hadn't been any recent killing here, but I'd sing of what I saw, of what I'd smelled and tasted, and of what I knew. I swam past the nest that had been our home. Now it was someone else's. Fry flashed outside, like light in the atmosphere. Staggered at being born.

92

They regarded me just as we had the crazed Banjxa soldier. I shouldn't have said a word. The fry flittered around me like light, or multitudes of uncountable smelt. They'd never seen a *yc* with markings like the ones on my chest, and naturally they were curious. Their parents hadn't seen a Gjala with my markings either, but they recognized I was one of them. Or at least I used to be. No doubt the parents could still taste me inside their nest. That had to frighten them.

Both approached me with their teeth bared. The fry showed their teeth too, an act of pure imitation. They weren't large or strong enough to pierce my skin, but I knew the circumstances would complicate quickly if I hurt any of them by accident. Suddenly, I was covered. Their fry were my skin, bubbling across it.

Should the parents have known me? I didn't know them. Maybe they'd arrived from another camp while I was gone, but I couldn't think about that now. I shook, to see if that would send any of them tumbling off. I shook again. Some were even in my mouth. They'd gone from sparks of light to smelt to sea lice. They could bite just hard enough to hold on, and so that I would feel them. But of course I could hear and smell them too—the flap and flutter of their tails and fins, covering me like algae.

You couldn't see the markings on me now. Did that count as camouflage? No, because their parents kept charging toward me. No sooner had I arrived than I fled. But their fry clung to me. And their parents tried.

I was a trail of glittering fry, a shooting star deep beneath the surface. I'd survived enough Banjxa attacks to imitate some of their moves, and that let me evade them. But the parents kept charging toward me, the mother stopping periodically to herd her dislodged babies back to their nest. Then she'd regroup and charge at me again. Would they ever catch me? No. But I'd have to keep moving.

I looked at the nest with longing. I couldn't stay.

I had reached the other side of our camp when I finally stopped swimming. Other *yc* were gathered around, but they knew me. Gjila was there, too. This was the first time I'd seen him since I'd received the markings. He didn't know what they meant, and I wouldn't tell him. There were more important things to tell the Gjala now.

A few fry remained, lodged in my incisions. But we were all clinging on for dear life.

93

I wanted to tell them a storm was coming. I wanted to tell them it was already here. That it was swelling and surging and on its way, and there was no way to stop it. But there are things you say that sound too crazy, too exaggerated to believe. And then you're left believing nothing at all. Except for what you see.

They believed I'd gone crazy. To be honest, I believed that, too. The camp was how I'd remembered it, which meant it hadn't changed at all.

Or, the only thing that had changed in it was me.

I could close my eyes and pretend this was a different time. I could open my ears and hear the sounds I was used to. I could gulp the water and be succored by its distinctive taste (it tastes like the insides of all of us, which makes it comfortingly digestive). Then I spoke, and it couldn't have mattered less what I had to say.

"Killer," one of them said. "You found the creature. Did you kill it, too?"

94

Immediately, it occurred to me they might all attack. Even Gjila. That's how far I had sunk.

Of course, he wouldn't. Of all my siblings, he was the one I thought of as family. Forget about cousins. The Banjxa, Caavaju, Dilidi, and Ecdda were all cousins. The Akla, too. Cousins, you kiss and kill. But this was different. Not least of all because he was skilled at war.

And Gola was gone. Gjila was all that was left.

The last of the fry freed themselves from my incisions. They'd nibbled on the scabs, and now the cuts were gleaming. Gjila swam to my side. We could all taste the blood from my chest. I suppose that was distracting.

But I could smell the tiny Gjala, too. Now that I wasn't trying to evade them—the countless swarms, wriggling and flitting like protozoa—I could focus on their scent, which matched their parents'. It is a bouquet. As they fin, they propel their scent through the currents. It wafts.

I breathed it in. Ravaged by all I'd seen, I still smelled their brood. And because you swallow what you smell, I had their taste. You don't talk about that, though, for even in the face of horrors we avoid what is unseemly.

That's what they must have thought of me.

Would they hear my story? Or not exactly my story, because those have beginnings and middles, and second and third beginnings, before their ends. Just like our songs. But there would be no end to mine, because nothing was finished, except for how we'd lived.

In the land creatures' world, are there animals with empires that last forever? Because if arthropods can live outside the water, I'd bet on them.

The attack was swift. The Banjxa, Ecdda, Caavaju, and Dilidi rained on us, like water on the surface. Each drop, or warrior, a single attack.

Rainwater is lifeless, saltless. Poison. The ocean surface doesn't welcome its arrival. Sometimes there is lightning. Or there is darkness. But both of those are just distractions. Then the rainfall comes. It seems insipid at first, until the algae spreads.

That's how it was with us. The fighting seemed trivial when it started, when it was only skirmishes. Like rain, you wouldn't call it an invasion. Compared to the land creature's discovery, what's a little violence? All of us are born with teeth. There's violence in our world every day, and we know not to think too much about it, because then you can't think about anything else. But the rifts had grown. The membranes covering us had split into pieces. When mucus tears, infections get in.

The purpose of violence is to share it. And then to let it multiply and spread. They were a rain of soldiers. A flood. They were a streaming churning crashing surge. They came at us from all directions.

We fought back. All of us. Including the fry. (Now that they weren't swarmed on me, I could see they stayed together, as a family.)

But we were alone. None of the Akla swimmers had survived the trip back to our camp. I called to them in the open sea, but it wasn't a song. Just broken notes, appeals to ghosts.

I recognized some of the Caavaju swimmers. They were captains Gjila and I had met long ago, when we still had faith in niceties like sardines and kelp. Now they were metamorphosing as they attacked, switching genders back and forth, as quick as the turns of a soldierfish school, as fast as blood can mix into ocean and turn blacker and angrier and lonelier as it sinks, evading our teeth and tails as their bodies shrank or swelled and their contours changed each time we lunged, so that we'd only slice and bite at *da'nāhai*, the empty water. But even more, it was meant to unnerve us. And to dazzle us, so that our muscles and bones would also fit their teeth. Their whole bodies were lures, stupefying and agitating us the moment they struck. As they attacked, I heard the Caavaju swimmers seething, disgust resonating through their own songs: "Wipe them out . . . everything. Whatever the ocean didn't put there. Everything that tastes like sadness. Whatever doesn't move." Of course, the Caavaju were a family, too. They dive-bombed our structures, the nests we'd made with enterprise and imagination. And hope. And then they dive-bombed us, too.

95

I meant this as a love story, and look where it is now. Where all of us are. The Banjxa, Caavaju, Dilidi, and Ecdda attacked in waves. And relentless swells. When you see the vents on the ocean floor spewing lava into the silent black, it's a sign that not all violence has personality. But that doesn't make it less effective. Once the Caavaju soldiers stopped singing and their genders no longer mattered, their attacks became twice as brutal. The strategy we'd used in the battlefields—our giant spheres of gyrating rings—didn't work in our camps, among the nests we had begun building with stones and shells, or with the Gjala who didn't know the formations. It would be simple to chant this as a song of sadness, but here is what I prefer to say: once you were my rainwater, too. You were poison and pure. Delicate as a drop, and delirious in volumes. But you weren't supposed to become the entire ocean.

When we love, is that something we each decide, or does it happen to you, like getting pulled away by the tide? We fall in love, and then don't know whether to ascend or sink. But when you love someone who dies, are you supposed to turn those feelings off, cut them off like a tail, wondering if one day they'll grow back, and how those new ones will appear? If you love someone else after that, do you use the same feelings, or do you need to create new ones? Does each love need to be an invention?

We all have the ocean in us, but we have other things too, and that is why we are different. I loved you with all I was, and all I am, and with all my scars. I love you that way now too, but since you're no longer alive it means it's all inside my head.

And yet the ocean's you. It is all of us. I know that with every breath. We touch each other's hearts and skin and loins. We touch our own. When we do, that emotion is in our minds, the only place it ever is. You're not just dependent on another's touch, their dedication or availability. We're not supposed to talk about those things in the middle of war, but shouldn't you before you die? I won't get another chance. Our relationship was made of many things, including everything that was unsaid. There is beauty in the world when you let it in, and we're fortunate that it seeps into all our spaces.

The attacks were relentless. Once, we could use their voices to plot their course, but now when we finally heard them, they were already at our backs and hearts.

I know you're there. I can smell and taste you. We resisted with all the strength we had. Gjila led our defense, and there was no one better. They destroyed our homes. And when they did, we picked up the rubble and used it to batter them as they had us, and they were right, you could do violence that way. (Yes, they destroyed the nest that once was ours.) But we were outnumbered, even in our own camps. I can't say by how many. I couldn't count the fry. But I know that there were less.

I counted their parents.

Now I'd prefer not to say.

And yet. I could smell you. Your scent was stronger. You filled the ocean. I breathed you amid the blood, amid the gravelly remains of homes and bones. I could smell your flesh. Almost taste it, and the more I sipped, the stronger it was. You were you, but a thousand of you. Or a million. Until you *were* the ocean, and I was pretty sure others could smell and taste you, too. Maybe they didn't know the scent—the history and peculiarities of it, and the way you shivered then as we watched the spawn—but they could smell something new and magical and magnificent and fierce, and whatever bafflement they sensed would be mixed with fear and hope, and maybe also pride and the squid-ink shame of having to fight for their lives when once we had another way . . . But that bafflement: it trickles through your eyes and skin, until it bathes and stings and tosses you from the insides out, until you can't recall your depth or whether you're rising or sinking. Then others stopped fighting and thrashing and gorging. Even the neckless sharks. Because like I said, you were poison. Perfect and overpowering. And then you were here.

The first soldiers appeared by the hundreds, and then they surged by the tens of thousands. I could taste and smell them, but now I could hear and feel them too, the way they moved the water as they swam, the vibrations and sounds around them, the whipping of their tails. The magnetic charges in the ocean, each one an insistent growing spark. And then I could see them, too. We have so many ways of deciphering the world around us that we don't rely on our eyes. The butterflyfish with their stupid spots know how easily eyes can be fooled. It is shameful to live your life inside a lie.

But, yes, I could see them. A phalanx of *yc* charging toward us. And they were you. They smelled of you. And tasted of you. And both that taste and smell grew and multiplied as they neared, and then they were here, attacking. At the Banjxa, Caavaju, and Dilidi throats. And at the Ecdda tails, swarming them until they bit and tore them off, and you had to wonder if a full-sized tail slapping at nothingness as it whirled and sank counted as a separate creature.

The Banjxa, Caavaju, Dilidi, and Ecdda fought back, and we fought back too, and then there were the sharks, and old alliances fell and the sharks only wanted to feed. When these *yc* were hurt, I smelled you even more. I smelled your insides pouring into the ocean, and your pain, because the taste of their blood was the taste of you, the you I'd chewed and swallowed once. But it was also me.

Then Gola arrived in the middle of the battle, and I felt myself go translucent for him.

96

He waited until my skin had turned back to opaque. It was the first time I'd changed for anyone, including you, and even in battle it was surprising and embarrassing. But Gola had known me since I was a fry.

"I went to find them."

The soldiers remained in tight formations. It was hard for the others to pick them off.

"The Fantaskla."

I looked at him.

"I knew their scent. You know it, too."

I did.

"You're not alone," Gola told me.

I told him, "I have you, too."

He told me of his hunt. By himself for all of it. The loneliness of being a single creature in the vastness of the ocean, bobbing up and down with his damaged swim bladder. The resolution, and the self-doubt. And the taste and scent. He'd held on to those for all this time, which was all my life. He swam with his mouth open. There was water to cover.

Oceans. Oceans. Seas.

Like me, he was lost. Or was he?—I don't know what's true. Both of us were grabbing at the past, or trying to. But Gola's efforts had a purpose.

Had he known about them all this time? Even if he'd only suspected, that would have been a thing to say. The Fantaskla aren't a phantasm. They are you. They are yours. Your flesh. Maybe they are somewhere out there in the ocean, in the world. And I am going to look.

Once they were embryos in the currents, too small for anyone to taste.

"You'd already lost everything," Gola said. "You had a place. A tribe. Did you need to lose any more?"

But now? Were we saved? Maybe. I felt gratitude, but also abandonment, even rage.

Yes, even with the Fantaskla around me.

The battles continued. In our camp, and in others. Across the oceans and the seas. In our world, dying is a natural occurrence, so it never will be surprising. But the ruthlessness and profusion of it were, because every life and death is distinct. Maybe the creatures on land are numb. They live without salt getting in their wounds. But here the end was everywhere you smelled and heard and gasped and looked. Until the ocean was water, minerals, blood. And it throbbed with the violence of the fighting. None of us can swim backward, no matter how fast we flick our fins.

Did it matter now in the face of so much death that I had my family? Was that supposed to be enough?

97

The ocean throbbed and pulsed. Concussed. You had to swim into the farthest, most isolated caves if you didn't want to feel it—and then squeeze into their smallest nooks. Many of the smaller fish, the herring, snappers, and fusiliers, were disoriented enough they plowed into rocks. You would see them with cuts across their faces, their dumb and unmovable expressions belying their astonishment and quiet humiliation. They'd counted on us to keep the order, so you could sense their disappointment. The larger fish, the jacks and tuna, stayed in deeper, open water, but they'd tumble out of formation when they tried to school. The billfish picked them off, but they had accidents, too. To see a swordfish impaled on another's bill is unnerving. There's no way to pull it off, and with the added weight and mass, they both mostly spiral down, in a paroxysm of flailing.

The sea cucumbers were blithe, except when they were hit. Then there was no end to their complaining.

The fighting wore on until it became the ocean's normal. Our normal. For a while, the Fantaskla held the others off. We teamed together. There was satisfaction in fighting with family by my side. We knew each other's smells, and we understood them. But we were not invincible. So we learned how each other tasted. I don't know if I was supposed to care less or more when one of them died, compared to the rest of us. All life seems important.

The land creature's life must have been important, too. Even if we can't know how it felt. About itself, or the others it resembled. I don't know if other creatures in the world are able to experience love, or if they just put on a show until they get the things they want. I suspect many crab species are like that.

I used to think we were different, or even better, but I am less inclined to believe that now. I can't even figure my own self out.

So I fought. All of us did.

What we lacked as two tribes we found as three. The Akla fought beside us, covered in glyphs—as I was now—their adolescents screeching. The Fantaskla didn't know what to make of them, but the Fantaskla remained a mystery, too. They didn't talk much. They watched us intently. They didn't differentiate between their females and males. They didn't need to change their genders.

Their adolescents didn't scream.

Aaa battled by my side. We didn't speak much either. Sound travels easily in the ocean. I've already said there can't be whispered secrets. Not if others are near.

We didn't require many words. You don't need them to fight. They expose your trajectory and location. Your intent.

And maybe, if we are to admit it, intention isn't always clear. It is grains of sand scooped up from the ocean floor, and when there are too many of them in the water, they block everything else out.

You were never returning. Gola did. Our offspring did. Their offspring, too. Generations can be born in the gaps between teeth. But you wouldn't. You'll always be inside these waters, and inside of me. Inside my thoughts and bones and voice. But I know that's not enough. The ocean is many things, so it will never be a single mineral or a song. Not if it needs to be life-sustaining.

I watched Aaa strike and tear. She'd threatened me the first time we met and never retracted her warning: "If a Gjala mates with an Akla, we'll kill you all." But we were all dying now, Gjala, Akla, and Fantaskla, and Banjxa, Caavaju, Dilidi, and Ecdda too, and there weren't many words present. Maybe words were our past.

Maybe I'll save my words for you, except for the ones written on my chest. Those you don't ever have to speak.

One day, perhaps, we'll have new tribes. But no matter where we go, despite the cultures we create and languages we use, we say the same things, filled with beauty, hope, and mistrust.

98

When we found the land creature, it seemed piteous and miraculous. That's what all of us thought. It was easy to mistake consensus for communality or shared convictions. You can do anything you like in the ocean with a shell or a stone. We know that. But the creature's discovery pushed us in directions we had never needed to explore. Its body seemed so frail. So ill-suited to living in any realm. Did it need our embrace? We dissected it instead.

The ocean is perfect because it is the only one there is. Maybe our seas aren't all that exist on earth, but they are all that matter. The rippled underside of the surface is a flimsy sheath, a warning for us to stay away. But there's no way to prevent others from falling or diving in. The petrels and shearwaters know this. The dolphins and whales flirt with the sky as well, but they always end up coming back. They never talk to us about what they see on land. I don't think that's even where they go.

When I pulled the creature from the rift, it had slipped through the last luminescence of the shallow zones to our world. Our ocean had bathed it and softened its skin. It was swaddled by sand. And it was repulsive.

It's easy to unite around something you despise, or at least that turns your stomach. But the land creature wasn't our enemy. It was already dead. Plus, the enemy of my enemy may still be something you shouldn't eat. Hate and nausea are funny things. They don't make you feel good about anything. Not yourself or one another. You'll never be able to rely on them to bind you together. There are better glues in the phospho-proteinaceous secretions of sandcastle worms or in the cement that oozes from behind a barnacle's eyes before adhering to its forehead.

Then there was envy. For what we imagined the creature could do with those limbs. Yes, there were animals among us who could move shells and small pebbles along the ocean floor—shrimp and crabs and fish—but none who could move big ones, or had thought that worth doing. Certainly we never had.

Did we need to now? Even before we started to build, we discovered we could use the stones and shells to make patterns and designs. Just like the white-spotted puffers, who make their nests in the sand. No male would think to copy another's and then pass those designs off as his own, except as a show of sarcasm. Besides, you find different sediments and topography where you build, so no two constructions can be the same. A lot of that is chance, but the rest is how you react to what's before you. We'd also always had love, which is the ultimate form of self-expression, even among the Ecdda. And so are songs— my point is we weren't stymied. But suddenly that wasn't enough. True, the miserable or unlucky don't necessarily find love, but they can sing about wanting it instead. That is also a chance for beauty.

But once you decide something's missing from your world, foundations start to fall apart.

There were many reasons for our rupture. Everything ruptures. Even in the ocean, where water has the tendency to push things together. Even after they're roiled and tossed apart.

But there was more to it than that. There has always been the ocean, since it is impossible to conceive of existence without the water. But water isn't all there is. We are surrounded by the remnants of the brilliant corals and fissures and gravity and skeletal life. There are hydrothermal vents hissing sulfur and bubbling with bacteria. There are trenches, and somewhere even deeper inside them there is fire and magma and the planet's core. There are places where the world is frozen and smoldering at the very same time, separated only by molecules that jump back and forth between them, and somehow there is existence and survival there, half death, half life, something that is neither of those or both. The world has been like that forever, which is as long as any of us can remember. We talk about Ooo, our ur-octopus, but the ocean goes back further.

To the beginning. When atoms mixed and molecules formed, and life on land wasn't plausible. I don't know how leaving the ocean ever seemed like something to consider. Our songs begin and re-begin. Each time there are verses, bridges, and refrains. But there is only one end, when you close your mouth. When you clench your teeth.

I don't think the land creature is new or that it has recently evolved. Maybe it needs to evolve some more. I don't know what kind of song it is—if it is one or many. The universe is ocean, pouring in all directions. It is possibility, even the most unlikely ones. Without gravity there is nothing to keep the water in place. All the universe is water, but the air above the ocean's sheath is water that is so diluted it's become a barrier to reaching the other parts. We see the stars, the luminescence of the creatures there, and maybe also the magma and the fire visible through the depths of its different zones, and the sprays of surf and steam on those planetary surfaces, and perhaps we would be comfortable there and even happy. If only we could get there, find some way to swim to the rest of the aqueous realm. We know the universe isn't land, or it would be a single ragged sprawl of stone that bubbled and stretched in all directions, and there wouldn't be room in the universe for anything else. So the land animal ended up where it always would. Among us.

Still, it had those limbs! And all our world's perfection didn't have ones like those. The possibilities they brought! Ooo would have moved stones, and giant ones. But it would have known when not to.

Those limbs, those tools—with their clutching, wiggling, grabbing ends, so easily detached from the body with just a tug—must keep the land creatures focused on building and destroying. So much to keep in their minds. So much to distract them. They must have lost their inner lives, and the meaning and understanding of all the things that make us who we are. That's what happened to us. What were we supposed to do with the vast seas of possibility the creature inspired? If the ocean is perfect, you can't change it to make it better. You can only make it different, but then you'd become different, too. Of course, the Caavaju already believed they were perfect, so any changes to their world would be a diminution. There was unquantifiable arrogance in believing that, but it didn't matter either way. They flow between genders, but they mean it as mesmerizing violence.

If the world became better, it meant it had problems that we hadn't been able to face—and not all of us have faces. Faces are supposed to demonstrate evolution. Do all land animals have faces? I doubt it.

If the world became worse, then shame on us. Because we destroyed it. You can't put a shell back together. Or a hope.

But the likeliest thing is that the world became better for some and worse for others, and a lot of that depended on what you wanted, your tenacity, and your luck.

We fought about what the creature was and what it meant. Our tribes were irreconcilable. Even those who were convinced the limbs were designed for peaceful and constructive ends were capable of inflicting harm in all the traditional, instinctual ways. So this is when our talk of places that were too cold and deep became trivial, because there was no place for us to go.

And when I talk about what the creature meant, let's be clear: I mean what it meant *to us*.

Yes, we were the victors. The Gjala, Akla, and Fantaskla united. In the sense that we united to kill the others.

I think the Fantaskla will always seem strange. Maybe more than any of our tribes, they understand the solitariness of survival. When Gola found them, they'd reproduced and enlarged like a jellyfish, without thoughts of love—neither bogged down nor enriched by it, until their bodies were only the ocean, with all its force and emotionlessness, and maybe that's why I can't recognize them, even if I know they're me.

We stopped visiting the canyon, and we stopped visiting the tomb. How could it be a place of peace? A place of common good, a place of meaning? A place where we celebrated ourselves, amid the streams and currents that had once wrapped around us, until they felt like an all-encompassing embrace? The place where we found the creature. A place of refuge.

Without the free movement promised by the water, the land creature must have felt trapped inside its world. Did it scramble across the stones and mud to scale its peaks, sniff the air for possibility, and jump? Cast itself into whatever openness lay before it and think, *I hope this is enough.* I'm not sure the Banjxa and the Caavaju didn't believe in building, as much as they didn't see a reason to or want to. To be fair, they didn't claim the appendages were for reaching into other creatures' mouths and tearing out their tongues, or the endless pounding that had pushed us into the Akla camp. But they showed us how they could be bent around a rock or broken shell, so that the swinging limb could cause even more damage. The first time I saw a sea cucumber severed in half and oozing life, I didn't need more convincing. It's hard to imagine they used those limbs just to cut and break things apart, when they could build storehouses, nests, cities, walls. But perhaps they'd use scratches and scores as a way of marking what terrain was theirs, as the Akla mark their bodies. And also mine.

The fighting wouldn't really ever end among our tribes. Victory is parasitic. Once you take another's nest, you can always say that once it was yours. You feed on that. It becomes your history and then your future. We live farther apart from one another now, wary that one of us will devise a new strategy and the fighting will become ever fiercer. And it will continue to spread.

All the water is connected. There is a single ocean, even if we have turned it into many. It will take two thousand years for the ocean to return to what it was. Or a hundred. Until then, we will be the scattered schools of the convinced. And unconvinced. But sometimes we wonder: if the creature's limbs could be used for scratching meanings onto bodies or onto rocks, then perhaps those were markings on the scraps we removed from its body. Because when you rubbed the mournful ribs of the hulk that once served as our temple and moved away the silt, weren't those symbols on it the same? A broken shell, smaller matching crescents?

If I had those limbs, I think the most important thing would have been to hold on.

Part 4

99

2038: USS *Trinidad*, a 9,217-ton DDG-139 Arleigh Burke–class Flight III destroyer, transits the Palauan Exclusive Economic Zone in response to an attack on two Japanese patrol boats and an Australian frigate, 90 nautical miles east of Morotai Island, Indonesia. A Chinese-flagged research vessel, which has entered the EEZ without authorization, reports it is conducting storm avoidance, while surrounded by the carcasses of sharks. Seaman Apprentice Robert J. Krucyff, age 20, from Bayonne, New Jersey, is missing from the crew, believed to have fallen overboard in rough seas. He will be remembered for his contribution to this peace-building mission.

And for his love for the ocean.

Acknowledgments

We live on the planet's skin and look up at the stars. We fly thirty-six thousand feet into the sky, often without a second thought, sometimes several days per week. We imagine life in space.

When we're by the coast, we look out onto the water's surface, but it's only when we see a whale or dolphin breach it, or a fishing vessel chugging back to port with its catch, that there's any visual proof the ocean descends below us, also to some thirty-six thousand feet. Is the sky empty? Not really. But we know there are at least 240,000 species in our oceans, and likely 500,000 to 10 million more.

I was fortunate to write much of *Underjungle* in Hawaii, where I could penetrate the ocean's surface and find inspiration amid the frenetically calming life. I wrote the rest of it in New York City, in an apartment, where the remaining parts seeped and coursed into my mind.

I want to thank those who influenced me as the book's ideas began to gel, from dive friends in Hawaii (who often showed up with the tanks!) to ones I've met on assignments to other coastlines and beyond. Learning to free dive with Kirk Krack and his Performance Freediving International team a decade ago, also in Hawaii, for an article in *The Atlantic* afforded me new reporting skills, plus a new way to think about being underwater. Two years later, on the Caribbean island of Petit St. Vincent, Richard C. Murphy of

Jean-Michel Cousteau's Ocean Futures Society introduced me to the idea of coral reefs as cities; then I read his *Coral Reefs: Cities Under the Sea*, and that idea sank in even more. Likewise, I was impacted and inspired by Jonathan Balcombe's *What a Fish Knows: The Inner Lives of Our Underwater Cousins*, Eugene H. Kaplan's *Sensuous Seas: Tales of a Marine Biologist*, and Neil Shubin's *Your Inner Fish: A Journey into the 3.5-Billion-Year History of the Human Body*, and by Rachel Carson's *The Sea Around Us* even before that. But my start was with the Sea-Monkeys I had as a boy. It didn't matter if they were actually brine shrimp and they didn't resemble the frolicsome creatures from the comic-book advertisements. It was fiction.

Special thanks go to my readers Paula de la Cruz, Caroline Friedman Levy, Sarah Gold, Andreina Himy, Veerendra Lele, Steve Mankoff, and Jeremy Mindich for their sage and surprising comments, which mostly soaked in. Additional thanks to Chris Heiser at the Unnamed Press, who prodded me toward new depths and truths, and to Pamela Malpas of the Jennifer Lyons Literary Agency for championing this story. Pamela, you are a splash of wisdom, terry-clothed with keenness.

This is a novel not just about the ocean, but about love, loss, and war. Maybe they are not our planet's universals, but they are ours. Paula has taught me much of what I know about the first. We all must accept the second and do whatever we can to find solutions to the last. Our world has changed. We must change, too.

Might as well make it sooner.